Newly estranged from Donna, The Introvert is selected as one of twelve jurors on a notorious murder trial, forcing him to navigate a litany of uncomfortable social interactions, this time with no avenue of escape. Equal parts harrowing and hilarious, The Introvert Bears Filthy Witness is the third entry in the life of one very anti-social and unexpected anti-hero.

Other novels by Michael Paul Michaud

Billy Tabbs (& The Glorious Darrow
The Introvert
The Introvert Confounds Innocence.

THE INTROVERT

BEARS FILTHY WITNESS

MICHAEL PAUL MICHAUD

A Black Opal Books Publication

GENRE: MYSTERY-DETECTIVE/SUSPENSE

This is a work of fiction. Names, places, characters and incidents are either the product of the author's imagination or are used fictitiously, and any resemblance to any actual persons, living or dead, businesses, organizations, events or locales is entirely coincidental. All trademarks, service marks, registered trademarks, and registered service marks are the property of their respective owners and are used herein for identification purposes only. The publisher does not have any control over or assume any responsibility for author or third-party websites or their contents.

THE INTROVERT BEARS FILTHY WITNESS
Copyright © 2021 by Michael Paul Michaud
Cover Design by Michael Paul Michaud
All cover art copyright © 2021
All Rights Reserved
Print ISBN: 9781953434111

FIRST PUBLICATION: JANUARY 2021

All rights reserved under the International and Pan-American Copyright Conventions. No part of this book may be reproduced or transmitted in any form or by any means, electronic or mechanical, including photocopying, recording, or by any information storage and retrieval system, without permission in writing from the publisher.

WARNING: The unauthorized reproduction or distribution of this copyrighted work is illegal. Criminal copyright infringement, including infringement without monetary gain, is investigated by the FBI and is punishable by up to 5 years in federal prison and a fine of $250,000. Anyone pirating our eBooks will be prosecuted to the fullest extent of the law and may be liable for each individual download resulting therefrom.

ABOUT THE E-BOOK VERSION: Your non-refundable purchase of this e-book allows you to one LEGAL copy for your own personal use. It is ILLEGAL to send your copy to someone who did not pay for it. Distribution of this e-book, in whole or in part, online, offline, in print or in any way or any other method currently known or yet to be invented, is forbidden without the prior written permission of both the publisher and the copyright owner of this book. Anyone pirating our eBooks will be prosecuted to the fullest extent of the law and may be liable for each individual download resulting therefrom.

IF YOU FIND AN EBOOK OR PRINT VERSION OF THIS BOOK BEING SOLD OR SHARED ILLEGALLY, PLEASE REPORT IT TO: Susan at skh@blackopalbooks.com

Published by Black Opal Books http://www.blackopalbooks.com

DEDICATION

For the weirdos

PART ONE
THE TRIAL

1. The Accountant
2. The Baker
3. The Dentist
4. The Retired Policeman
5. The Dancer/Shelley's Sister
6. The Garbage Collector
7. The Student
8. The Old Woman
9. The Introvert
10. The CEO
11. The Nurse
12. The Adventurer

Chapter 1

D id you really think you were going to get away with it?"

It wasn't much of an opening sentence. It was a trite thing for a policeman to say, and it was also an unfair question, because either which way you answered it would make you look guilty. So, I decided not to answer it at all, which seemed like the smartest thing to do, and the only reasonable alternative.

It also wasn't much of an interrogation room. The chairs were comfortable and the temperature was mild, and I didn't even see a hot lamp or a phonebook anywhere.

It was the young, clean-shaven policeman who'd asked the question because the older one with the mustache had just then entered the room. The two of them proceeded to ask me a series of pointed questions about the man's death, including whether it was premeditated and such, but there really wasn't much that I could say. That was when the older, mustached officer left the room.

"Real emotional type, aren't you?"

He wasn't much of a police officer. He was wearing bright red suspenders and colored socks that all seemed too fashionable for someone investigating such a serious crime, and his tone was mocking and unprofessional.

The fact of the matter was that I wasn't sad that he was gone, only I didn't want to confirm it, because I felt that might make them even more suspicious than they already were.

"It is unfortunate that he was killed," is all I said.

"Unfortunate you killed him, you mean?"

"No," I said, only then he leaned in really close.

"So you don't think it's unfortunate that you killed him?"

He was trying to twist my words around as police officers often did.

"I did not say that I did any such thing," I said.

"Yeah, and you sure as hell didn't say you didn't," he said, as he slammed his fist down onto the table.

That was when the older officer with the mustache came quickly back into the room and said, "Whoa, whoa," while guiding him aside. Then he came back to where I was and slowly took the seat beside me.

"You have to forgive my partner," he said. "He's just pretty wound up about this one. You understand?"

He said it really softly and gently as his partner stewed just a few feet away, pacing back and forth beside the wall.

I said that I understood, and then he asked me if he could get me anything, like a glass of water or a cigarette.

I believed them to be engaging in the "good cop, bad cop" routine, which was a psychological ploy police officers often utilized that was meant to lower the suspect's defenses, such that it would engender trust between the suspect and the officer showing kindness, and thus lead to quicker and more fulsome confessions. We used similar techniques in my company in order to sell vacuums, and while there were likely nuances between convincing a customer to purchase a new model vacuum cleaner versus convincing them to confess to murder, I felt that the underlying psychology was likely quite similar.

"I will take a cigarette," I said.

"Fuck this guy's cigarette," said the young policeman, still pacing back and forth.

"We'll get you that cigarette," said the mustached officer, ignoring his younger counterpart. He stood up slowly and stepped out of the room, returning shortly with a pack of cigarettes and a lighter. He placed them both on the table in front of me with the lighter on top of the pack before he resumed his seat.

I hadn't actually wanted a cigarette. I'd only said that I did because he'd offered it, and I had seen this type of encounter many times on television and in the movies, and I felt that it was the appropriate response. Only now that he'd gone to the effort of obtaining them, I felt compelled for the sake of etiquette to remove one from the package and light it, so that's what I did.

I took a couple of puffs, but exhaled quickly. Then I watched as the smoke climbed toward the ceiling, wondering about what type of ventilation they had, and if we might be breaking any city by-laws.

The officer sat silently beside me for several more puffs, but finally he started to speak.

"It was the trial, right? Something about the trial, or maybe something that came up in the jury room?"

I didn't answer him right away, because I was still watching the ceiling as more smoke collected. I'd already been wondering if it might set off the smoke alarm, and perhaps even the sprinkler system, and if all of the prisoners might then have to be evacuated, and if that happened, I wondered if they would be free to walk around outside until the danger had passed, or if they would be kept shackled and guarded. And I wondered what they would do with the prisoners from solitary confinement, and if they would have to sit by themselves outside, and if so, what radius from the other prisoners would be required.

"We'll be speaking to the other jurors, of course."

Still I didn't respond, because by then I was thinking about how the firemen would probably have to come do a precautionary safety check if there was an evacuation, and it made me wonder if any of the prisoners might try to stow away on one of the fire trucks in order to escape, or how one of them might even try to subdue a fireman and take his uniform in order to blend in. Of course, it could also be a female prisoner trying to subdue a firewoman.

"Something happened between the two of you, didn't it?"

The officer drew my attention back to the moment, and I saw how serious his face was, and how much he truly wanted me to answer his questions. It was obvious that they wanted to know what happened to the man, and if I'd had any involvement in his death. Only at that point I wasn't thinking about murder, or vacuums, or even ventilation. At that point I wasn't thinking about much of anything at all. Except for one thing.

I was thinking about a number.

Chapter 2

"Two nine two five six seven!"

That was my jury number, which had just been called aloud by the court registrar. I'd been provided it when I'd registered that morning with the rest of the prospective jurors before we were all corralled into the courtroom.

It wasn't much of a courtroom. The inside was drab and dated and it didn't have any windows, but at least the pews were in good shape, if they even still called them that.

There were nearly two hundred of us to begin with. That's when the registrar lady put all of our numbers into a small metal cylinder and spun it around by the handle before drawing the numbers out one by one. In this way it was much like the lottery or bingo, except that you didn't actually want your numbers to be called out, nor would you jump out of your seat to yell a trite phrase in the event that it was, so I suppose in hindsight it wasn't much like those things at all.

I had tried to memorize my number very early and took pride in the fact that I could do so after less than a minute. Only, when the registrar called it out, I still glanced down at the paper to verify that I was correct. I'm not sure why I did it, only I think a lot of people probably did the same thing, which seemed not only unnecessary but to betray a level of insecurity. But what was done was done, so I figured there was no sense beating myself up about it.

I stepped into the witness box and looked at the judge. She was a middle-aged woman who seemed too young and too pretty to be a judge, only then I quickly recognized that this sort of thinking was a form of misogyny through preconceived stereotypes, and so I apologized to the judge for thinking it, only I did so quietly in my mind.

Two men were on trial for murder. One was black and one was white. The lawyer for the black man – Mr. Munroe – was allowed to ask a question about whether or not the prospective juror would be pre-disposed against his client based on the color of his skin. To me, this just seemed like he was drawing unnecessary attention to the obvious, and if someone was truly racist, they would likely not be inclined to say so, but he asked the question all the same.

"Sir," he said, standing behind a wooden lectern, "would your ability to judge this case be affected by the fact that my client is of African-American descent?"

I didn't immediately answer, because by then I had reconsidered whether a racist person would invariably hide their racism, or if they might actually appreciate the opportunity to express it. I knew that some racist people were genuinely proud of their Aryan ancestry, even if they misunderstood what that actually meant, like they misunderstood most other things.

Finally, I said, "My best friend is black," and this was an easy statement to make because Gordon was indeed my best friend, even though the truth of the matter was that he was probably also my only friend. I hadn't known Gordon very long, but he treated me differently from the way most people did, and when Donna asked me to leave our home last week due to a simple misconception, Gordon had offered me a place to sleep.

"Although at first I wasn't sure he was sufficiently black to want to be called black," I added.

"'Sufficiently black'?" asked the defense lawyer, with a puzzled look on his face. That's when I saw Mr. Crooks' lawyer - who was seated next to his client and wearing a bolo tie - turn and smile arrogantly to the jury members who had already been picked ahead of me and were assembled in the jury box. I counted eight who'd been selected, and a number of them laughed when he did this. The person who laughed loudest was the fourth juror, who was a large balding man with a circumference of gray hair around the bottom of his head.

"Sir," said the judge, leaning in from her dais, "do you not want to serve on this jury?"

"I would prefer not to," I said. I said it because it was true, and in direct response to her question, only I saw her face turn ugly when I said it.

"And is there any particular reason why?"

There were actually many reasons why. Mostly it was because I didn't like to be around people more than I absolutely had to, and from what little I'd seen, the criminal justice system seemed like a place where you would be routinely forced to come into contact with people you would ordinarily do your best to avoid. But it wasn't just that. The fact was that Donna had recently asked me to leave the house because she incorrectly believed that I'd been having an affair with our neighbor, and I believed that serving on a jury would interfere with my efforts to regain her favor. Also, I sold vacuum cleaners for a living, and I couldn't imagine I'd be able to sell very many from within a courtroom. I thought of all this in my mind but didn't say any of it out loud, and before I could say anything at all the judge said, "All right then," only she didn't leave it at that.

"You do realize that this is your civic duty?" she said sternly.

"Yes," I said.

"And that many would deem it an honor to serve their community."

I hadn't thought of it that way, and I was even prepared to say that it probably would be an honor, only before I had a chance to say how much of an honor it would be, she started talking again.

"Sir, I expect from this point on that you will refrain from any efforts to evade jury duty," then she turned quickly toward the lawyer with the bolo tie and told him to ask his question again.

I'd found in life that the more you didn't want to spend time with a woman the more she wanted to spend time with you in return, and from what I had seen so far, it seemed like judges acted the same way about prospective jurors. Though I suppose it could have just been female judges.

"I'll ask the question again," said the defense lawyer for Mr. Monroe, politely repeating his earlier question, "If you are selected for this jury would your ability to judge this case be affected by the fact that my client is of African-American descent?"

I thought I'd answered this question sufficiently before with my earlier answer, only this time I simply said, "No," in an attempt to be more direct, and this seemed to be the answer they were looking for because then the judge said "Counsel?" and I saw both the prosecutor and the two defense lawyers look at each other and nod their heads.

"Unless you have any great objection?" asked the judge, leaning in toward me.

I figured this was a rhetorical, sarcastic question made at my expense, so I just walked over to the jury box where I stepped inside and sat down in the ninth chair.

Chapter 3

Since I was the ninth juror selected, they only had to pick three more, plus two alternates.

The tenth person selected was a man in his forties with a fancy blue suit and what looked like shiny leather alligator shoes, though I suppose they might have been snake. He was apparently a CEO for a Fortune 500 company. I knew this because he relayed this to the court at the first opportunity, which to me made him look even more insecure than when I had looked down to re-check my identification number.

The eleventh juror was a female nurse aged about forty. She was tall and attractive, and I figured that if I had to go through some medical ordeal that I would probably want someone like that as my nurse, assuming she was competent.

The twelfth and final juror simply called himself an "adventurer." I had never heard of this profession before, but since the lawyers didn't ask him to clarify what it meant, he took the last seat just as quietly as I had, and nothing more was said about it.

I would soon learn that the first eight jurors were, respectively; an accountant, a baker, a dentist, a retired policeman, a dancer, a garbage collector, a student, and an old woman. Though I suppose I didn't need to learn the old woman was an old woman because unlike my blind friend Gordon, I didn't have any problem seeing obvious things.

Once we'd been selected, we each had to swear an oath on the bible, or if you weren't superstitious, to just promise to tell the truth. Then the judge said that we should retire into a room while she talked with the lawyers and that we might use the opportunity to get to know one another better. They had told us at the outset that the trial could take the better part of a month, and while I found this sort of lengthy forced social interaction to be a significant failing of our government, I figured there wasn't much I could do about it, so I went along with the jury attendant who escorted us all into a room with a long rectangular table and twelve chairs, and a water cooler in the corner. We had only just stepped inside when juror number four, who was the retired police officer, approached me from the side.

"That routine usually work for you?" he said.

I asked him what he meant by it.

"You know, the idiot bit. Fumbling around like you don't know what you're saying."

"I answered the questions honestly."

"Yeah, I'm sure you did." Then he moved closer into my space and said, "Look, I didn't lay my life on the line every day for forty years just so the next generation could come around and piss all over it."

He gesticulated toward the floor with his hands as he talked. "So, how about you show a little respect from now on, hey chief?" Then he patted me on my chest, but he did it hard enough to convey to me that he wasn't being friendly, and then he walked away.

He wasn't much of a retired police officer to be saying these things. I also wondered why he'd just called me "chief" because that was a term usually used for aboriginal or indigenous people, such as the tall actor who'd helped Jack Nicholson play basketball.

I had also learned from a child psychology magazine that bullies on playgrounds tended to pick on the quiet, smaller kids, and that if you don't stand up to them early, they would continue to do so and things would only get worse. I had recently experienced this with my own son, Toby, who found the courage to oppose his own bully, and even if Toby's chosen tactics were somewhat excessive, I still felt there was enough in that response that might apply to the present situation. So, I immediately walked toward the retired police officer. He was standing talking with another one of the jurors, only I didn't look closely enough to see which one.

"I did not appreciate the way you just spoke to me," I said. I said it because it was true.

He turned around slowly and looked me in the eyes.

"What's that, fella?"

I knew that he'd heard me.

"I did not appreciate the way you just spoke to me," I repeated. "And it would be best if you did not touch me again."

He was initially taken aback by my response, only then he scoffed, or at least made a sound resembling a scoff, and said, "Oh, would it?"

"It would," I said, and this was true too. While I could often contain my scary thoughts if I engaged my breathing exercises, these feelings became harder to control when people touched me in ways that I did not approve of. And I felt that if he continued to touch me as he had before that there was a fair chance the lady registrar might soon be putting names and numbers into a small metal cylinder for my own trial.

"Now there's no reason to get excited, boys."

This was when I first noticed that it was the last jury member—the Adventurer—with whom he'd been speaking. He was about middle age with dirty blonde hair and tanned skin, and he looked very much like the kind of person who went about hunting crocodiles or spelunking in caves. He even had an accent that might have been Australian, though I suppose it also could have been from New Zealand.

"The nerve of this guy," said juror number four, speaking to the Adventurer.

"Look, this is a bit of an unusual situation for most of us," said the Adventurer. "Maybe it's got some of us on edge. Maybe just be good to settle in easy, how's that, gents?"

Before either of us could answer, the old woman appeared, took me by the arm, and gently led me away.

"You just come with me, young man," she said, stepping us toward the other side of the room. "I heard the way that he was talking to you," she added, after stopping a safe distance away. "Just a terribly rude man. You shouldn't let him get a rise out of you."

"I suppose not," I said, and by then my emotions had started to settle.

"And from the sounds of it, we're all stuck together now, so we might as well make the best of it."

The things she was saying were the sort of things that Donna and I had said to Toby when he was having trouble at school with his own bully, and I immediately recognized how some lessons were universal.

"But if he gives you any more trouble, you just let me know," she said, and she squeezed my hand as she said it.

The woman must have been in her mid to late eighties, and though I usually wasn't comfortable with people touching me without my permission, there was something different about old people with wrinkled skin.

After speaking with her a while longer, I walked over to the water cooler and looked out at the others, which was something that I usually did at parties and gatherings, and apparently also in jury rooms. I soon noticed that the loudest three people were the retired policeman, the CEO, and the nurse, and it made me believe that these three people might have a disproportionate influence on the other members of the jury, as they appeared the most vocal and therefore possibly the pushiest. By contrast, the two quietest people, aside from myself, appeared to be the student and the baker. They were each off on their own minding their own business. The student, who was dressed in black clothing and had black hair and makeup, was reading a book called "Eat, Poop, Sleep," which was apparently a satirical book about a popular spiritual memoir that was later turned into a very unpopular movie. She looked to be about a third of the way through the book, and it made me curious about what page she was on, and even though I couldn't see the page numbers from where I was standing, my mind liked to fill in the gaps whenever possible, so it picked the number 171, which seemed about right and was at least enough to satisfy my curiosity in the moment.

After a few more minutes, the jury attendant returned and said, "I trust you all had a nice chat?"

I thought about telling him about my exchange with juror number four, only then I figured that his comment was likely more of a platitude than an actual inquiry, so instead I just filed out of the room with the rest of the jurors into the short hallway leading to the courtroom.

I was right behind the student as we went in, and then I started wondering how many pages in total there were in her book, and how much longer it would take her to finish it. I figured I would probably check in on her progress from time to time as the trial went along because that was the sort of stuff that I did and the type of stuff that made me happy, and the type of distracting thoughts that helped keep prospective juror names out of my own metal cylinder.

Chapter 4

Once we'd re-entered the courtroom, the judge read us some brief instructions about how to be jurors. Then she invited counsel to make their opening submissions.

The prosecutor was a woman just like the judge, which was only to say that she was a female of about middle age and she was working in a courtroom. She soon told us that the white gentleman, Peter Crooks, and the black gentleman, Sheldon Munroe, had broken into a fancy home last December and murdered a woman named Shirley Baker who was home alone with her dog while her husband was at a business meeting. Only she didn't actually mention the skin color of the accused parties like I just did in my mind, perhaps because Mr. Munroe's defense lawyer had already brought so much attention to it.

I immediately started thinking about how funny it was that one of the defendants had a name like Crooks, only I wasn't thinking about it being funny for very long because I recognized that this was quite a serious matter.

That was when I refocused my attention, and I heard the prosecutor say that Crooks and Munroe likely expected the home to be empty because they hadn't brought a weapon with them. She said this because Mrs. Baker's head was bashed in with a marble statue from the mantelpiece downstairs, which had been abandoned next to her body.

As the prosecutor outlined the gruesome details, I could see the look of horror on some of my fellow jurors' faces, which was a look I'd seen from other people in various circumstances when I would sometimes let my scary thoughts get the better of me. The only people who seemed unaffected by what was just said were jurors four and five, and while I understood how a retired police officer might be de-sensitized to hearing about violence, it seemed to be unusual for a dancer.

After the prosecutor finished her opening statement, both of the defense lawyers were given an opportunity to address us.

Mr. Crooks's defense lawyer went first. He was the smug man with the bolo tie who had smiled at the jury when Mr. Munroe's lawyer had introduced himself to me by asking if I was a bigot. He stood up rather forcefully, pushing his chair back sharply as he did, then exclaimed loudly that his client was innocent, in a tone that suggested not only sureness, but perhaps even outrage at the charges. As a result of this, I briefly thought that his client had been falsely charged, only then I remembered that this was likely a tactic most defense lawyers use, even when they knew their clients were guilty, so I silently vowed not to be fooled so easily by such tactics and to confine myself exclusively to the evidence as the judge had urged us to do.

The lawyer then stated that neither his client nor the co-accused had harmed the woman or the dog. This was the first time I heard that a dog had been harmed, and it immediately made me think about my own dog Molly, and how if someone broke into my home and harmed her that I would likely do whatever it took to find them and make them red and open. Mr. Crooks's defense lawyer then admitted that the men were guilty of burglary, but called them, "petty thieves," incapable of committing a heinous crime such as murder." Then he suggested that it was surely the victim's husband who had murdered the woman, and how the poor timing of their burglary made them "ready-made patsies."

Finally, Mr. Munroe's defense lawyer had his turn. He was younger and seemed much more professional than Mr. Crooks's lawyer because he walked up very calmly to the wooden lectern and reminded the jury that Mr. Munroe was merely alleged to be a party to the offence as he had driven them to the location in a van and waited outside while much of the burglary took place. He conceded that his client was a party to the burglary, acting chiefly as the lookout and the getaway driver. He asserted that Mr. Munroe had only gone inside for a short while to help Mr. Crooks carry out some of the larger items, which they later split up and sold. He added that there was no plan to harm anyone that night, and that his client did not see any other person in the house aside from Mr. Crooks.

In my view, each of these three scenarios seemed entirely plausible, only I wasn't in much of a mood to weigh the likelihood of each possibility as I was by then wondering what kind of dog it was, and how badly it had been injured. However, before I could think about it any further, the judge said that due to the lateness of the day, we would adjourn until the next morning when we would hear from the first witness.

As was the custom, everyone except the judge stood up as we were led out of the courtroom, down the back hallway, and into our jury room. Once there, the jury attendant said that we were all free to go, but to ensure that we were here no later than 9:30 a.m. the next day, and it was just a few minutes later that I was alone in my car where I did some of my best thinking, and in this case, much of my best thinking was about the dog.

Chapter 5

I returned home just in time for dinner.

It wasn't actually my home, but Gordon's home. He had invited me to live with his family until I had sorted things out with Donna, which was to say that things need not be all the way sorted out, with her helping me to achieve it and wriggling up close to my side, but at least sorted out well enough to allow me back into the house overnight, even if only on the couch.

When I'd told Gordon that I had started living out of a hotel he told me that I should just come live with him and Sharon and the kids. I'd initially found this offer strange, not because of his generosity, but because he hardly ever spoke about his family, so to me it was almost as if they weren't real people. Mostly we just talked about work, and whenever we did talk about other subjects, Gordon usually preferred social justice issues or other topics that were depressing and not likely ever to get better.

As it turns out, none of his family were dwarves or blind like Gordon was. This is not to say that I doubted they were his family, or suspected that his wife had had an affair, because they were still sufficiently black like Gordon was, and both of his kids called him, "Daddy," and there was nothing in their tone which suggested their use of that name was part of an elaborate ruse.

Their house had a finished basement with its own bathroom, so they invited me to move down there and sleep on the pullout couch, so starting last week that's what I did. The basement also had a telephone, so after I got in, I went downstairs to my room and called my real home, and Toby answered.

"Hi, Daddy," he said.

I said, "Hello, son," because he was indeed my son, and this was something I'd heard many fathers say in some of the old television shows I'd watched, and the children on television seemed to enjoy it.

"Are you coming home soon, Daddy?"

"I'm not sure," I said. I wasn't being coy or playing hard to get like women sometimes did with the men they liked, but the fact was that I simply didn't know the answer. Donna had wrongly suspected me of having an affair with our neighbor due to some marks she had observed on my body, and even though there was a mostly innocent reason why I had those marks, Donna had asked me to leave the home, and I had capitulated rather quickly. During the course of my relationship with Donna, I had learned that she was easily governed by her emotions, and while it could often be frustrating that she could swing from angry to sad to happy all very quickly and without much warning, I also thought that this might be one of the few times I might benefit from this condition. So I asked Toby if Mommy was home, and when he said that she was, I asked to speak to her.

It was nearly a minute before Donna came to the phone, and I quickly discerned that she had not sufficiently swung back to happy yet, based on the tone of her voice and the shortness of her answers.

"Toby would like to know when I will be home," I said.

"And what did you tell him?"

"I said that I did not know." I left off the extra part I'd been thinking about her shifting emotions, because I had found little benefit to vocalizing such things, no matter how true they were, and in fact it could often trigger another bout of the very same behavior.

"Well, that's good," she said.

"I have used most of my clothes," I said.

"Well, does Gordon have a washing machine?"

I admitted that he did, so she said nothing more on it.

"I would like you to know that I have not been unfaithful to you," I said. Then I heard a muffling on the other end before things got quiet. For a moment I thought that perhaps Donna had hung up me, but then she started speaking, and I could tell that she was crying.

"I want to believe you. I just don't know what to think."

"Perhaps you could just ask Hayley?"

Hayley was our neighbor, and the woman with whom Donna mistakenly believed that I had entered into an affair.

"I'm not sure that would be such a good idea," she said, only she didn't say why it wouldn't be. That was when I heard Toby in the background asking why she was crying, and Donna said she had to go, so I told her I loved her, but she just said, "Mmm-hmm," back and quickly hung up the phone.

After the call, I changed out of my work clothes, and it was shortly after this that Gordon arrived home. His wife ordinarily picked up the children from daycare, only today they were late, so Gordon and I convened in the kitchen where he offered me a beer.

Gordon and I sold vacuums. They were good vacuums with an excellent reputation, only today someone's vacuum had apparently caught fire, and rather than calling the customer service center as they were told to do, she had called Gordon directly, who was the salesman. Since I worked right beside Gordon, I knew that he often encouraged his customers to call him directly with any concerns, though it would seem that Gordon was less interested in this actually happening as he was in saying it to help secure the sale.

"Woman calls me, says she took it apart to clean it, I mean like all the way apart. Got tools and unscrewed everything. Then after putting it back together and turning it on, the damn thing started smoking."

"I see."

"So she tells me it's not supposed to do that, and I said, 'You're damn right it's not supposed to do that', and then she got upset with my language and said I wasn't being very sympathetic. So then I told her that maybe I'd have more sympathy if she hadn't have gone all MacGyver on the damn thing, and she didn't like that either."

Gordon was becoming animated as he spoke.

"Anyway, then she demands to speak to Frank, so I said 'sure' – and then Frank comes over to talk to me about it later, trying to coach me on better customer relations. So I ask Frank if he wants me to spend my time mollycoddling old bats who think they're the second coming of Thomas Edison, or if he wants me to spend it closing new sales, and of course, he didn't have anything to say to that."

Frank Peters was our boss, only I just called him Mr. Peters, and while I suspected that our company would generally frown upon this type of interaction with our customers, Gordon was also one of our best salespeople, and I'd found that the better someone was at their job was inversely proportional with how stringent the bosses would apply the rules.

Gordon was what some people called a "challenger" because he didn't have much patience for things that he didn't agree with. He also didn't have a problem expressing to people how he really felt, and while this level of heartfelt honesty might sometimes lead to tender moments between a father and a son, or a husband and a wife, it appeared a less successful strategy when speaking to a sixty-five-year-old woman who'd just frantically unplugged her vacuum cleaner lest she perish in a fiery blaze.

"We are taught that the customer is always right," I said.

"Not sure about that. Always an asshole, maybe."

"So what happened with the vacuum?" I asked, trying to re-focus the conversation.

"They sent someone out to her house. Turns out when she put it back together, she got a cat toy stuck in the machinery and it was catching fire on the inside. As if a catnip fucking mouse looks like a bolt or a screw. I don't have time for people's shit."

Gordon didn't say anything else, and I decided this was a good time to change the subject completely, so I told him about my first day at court, including the jury selection process, and how I got picked, and also about what happened with the retired police officer. I did not share anything about the case because the judge had told us not to discuss it with outsiders. Gordon said I did the right thing by confronting him, but then warned me that it might not be over.

"Cops always think they get the last word," he said. "They think they get to win every argument just because they have a badge."

"But he is retired," I said.

"You think that matters to him?"

I was thinking of what to say next when Sharon and the girls arrived home. Gordon's daughters both ran into the kitchen yelling, "Daddy, Daddy," and after giving him a hug, they came over and did the same with me. Then Sharon came inside and kissed Gordon hello, and as much as I was happy for Gordon, I couldn't help thinking of my own familial estrangement.

"You boys hungry?" she asked as she came into the kitchen and washed her hands. Sharon was always washing her hands and cleaning things around the house, both of which I found to be strong character traits. She also worked at one of the local animal shelters tending to sick and neglected animals and doing her best to find them homes, which was all to say that she was not only a clean person, but that she was also a good person.

We soon ate dinner around the kitchen table, and for a while I forgot about vacuums and juries and trial separations, and I just enjoyed the food that Sharon had made, only at the end I started to cough.

"You catch something?" asked Sharon.

I said that it was possible, because my throat had been scratchy the last couple days.

"It's not too drafty down there, is it?" she said, with a look of concern.

"No," I said. "Only I have been feeling tired lately, so perhaps I have worn myself out."

"I'm going to make you some tea," she said, standing up even before finishing the food on her plate. I saw Gordon give me a funny look as she walked over to the stove, only I didn't know exactly what the look meant, and I didn't ask.

A couple minutes later she came back holding a red mug, which she placed down on the table in front of me.

"It's got honey and lemon in it, too," she said.

That's when Gordon got the same funny look back on his face.

"You're not careful she'll adopt you," he said.

I understood Gordon to be joking as I was far too old for being adopted. Only I couldn't help but think that if I were to be adopted as an adult, I would not much mind if it were by a good, clean person like Sharon.

After drinking my tea, I went downstairs and sat on the pullout couch and watched some television. That was when I started wondering if it should still be referred to as a pullout couch if it wasn't pulled out yet, which it wasn't, only then I quickly concluded that it was probably still fair to call it that, even if slightly imprecise, so I didn't think about whether it should be called a couch or a pullout couch for very long.

Chapter 6

The next morning I arrived at the courthouse promptly at 9:15 a.m., because I wanted to ensure I was there at least fifteen minutes early, which was a business philosophy called "Lombardi time" that I had learned at my company. Our company was always teaching us trite business tricks like these, which they said would increase our productivity and engrain within us a professional edge that would benefit us in all aspects of our lives for years to come. In my experience, the company was less concerned with engraining within us a professional or any other type of edge, as much as they were concerned with engraining extra money onto their bottom line, only I figured that it couldn't hurt to go places fifteen minutes early, unless maybe by going early it caused you to get into a gruesome accident that you otherwise would have avoided, in which case it probably would hurt, and the pain might even be excruciating.

Unfortunately, I didn't feel any better than I did the day before, and in fact I felt worse. My throat had gone from scratchy to sore, and I was coughing more regularly, only I didn't want to bring this up to the judge because I felt like she was already irritated with me and figured she would think this was a new ruse to get out of jury duty, even if there hadn't been an original ruse to begin with.

After going through security the jury attendant led me into the jury room, where only one person had arrived ahead of me, so I decided to sit down beside her. It was juror number five, the dancer who hadn't appeared shocked by the allegations.

"Look at us early birds," said the dancer, also seated at the table. She was thin with bright red hair halfway down her back, and she looked to be in her early twenties.

"The early bird catches the worm," I said. I said it because it was a trite, common phrase, and I had read that using idioms was often a good way to break the ice with other people, only she just looked at me weakly after I said it.

Just then juror number two—the baker, a fair-skinned, obese man—entered the room and cheerily said, "Time to make the donuts!" as he walked in, which was originally from an old television commercial about a baker who had to get up early to make donuts for his customers, and had now become synonymous with being forced to get up early against your will.

He set the box on the table in front of us, so I selected one in order to be polite and also because they smelled delicious. The dancer sat quietly beside me as I consumed it, while the baker settled a few feet away with a newspaper.

Finally, she said, "So you're in sales, huh?"

"I sell vacuums," I said.

"You sell a lot?"

"I suppose I sell enough to keep my bosses happy and to provide for my family. Donna also provides for the family, but her salary doesn't provide as much."

"Is that right?" she said, and then she laughed as if maybe I'd said something funny, which is something that many people did when speaking with me, and something I had mostly gotten used to by that point in my life.

"And you are a dancer?" I said, because the court clerk had called out our job titles each time we had come forward to be asked if we were prejudiced. She nodded after I said it.

"That must be enjoyable work," I said.

She looked at me after I said it as if, perhaps, I wasn't being genuine, only the fact of the matter was that I figured dancing was an enjoyable form of employment, both because it was artistic and also because it involved exercise. I had read in a magazine that people who sat at desk jobs lived on average eight to ten years shorter lives than those who had active jobs, so that likely meant that juror number five would likely live eight to ten years longer than the rest of us, except maybe for the Adventurer.

Finally, she said that the work was enjoyable, but that some people didn't approve. To me this didn't make sense, because dancing had long been considered a wholesome activity, and an important part of art and culture, so I told her how a lot of people sing and dance on television, and how many of these were family features, and some were even cartoons. Only then she told me that her dancing wasn't so much stuff like that, as much as it was dancing around poles in dark places with her body naked and brushed with glitter, so then I had to concede that this was something I rarely saw in family programming, and certainly never from talking beavers or raccoons.

She laughed when I said it, and then I saw the expression on her face change to a much happier one.

"I'm trying to save for school," she said.

"I see."

"College is just so expensive."

"It is," I said. I said it because it was true.

"And I want to make something of myself, like my sister."

"What does she do?"

"Shelley is a police officer."

"I see."

I had spent my fair share of time around police officers in recent weeks, so something about her saying this unsettled me. Only then, just as quickly, I thought about how she hadn't reacted yesterday when the prosecutor had talked about the murder allegations, so I figured that maybe she had heard about this sort of stuff from her sister Shelley, or else maybe she had seen bad things as a dancer, so at least it felt good to have that part settled.

As we sat and talked, the other jurors filtered in, and I noticed right away when juror number four entered the room because he was just as loud as he had been yesterday, as if he wanted to ensure that the other people in the room knew that he had arrived. Then I saw him huddle up alongside the Adventurer just like he had yesterday, and he was still talking loud even though they were only a couple feet apart, and he would occasionally slap the Adventurer on the back or engage in some other physical way with him, and it made me uncomfortable just to see it.

"I saw how he spoke to you yesterday," said Shelley's sister. "You did a good job standing up for yourself."

I thanked her for the compliment.

"What an asshole," she said, still staring at him, only she said it quietly so nobody else could hear.

"My friend Gordon says that police officers think they get to have the last word and win the argument because they have a badge, even if they don't actually have a badge anymore."

"Yeah, there are some cops like that. Shelley calls them cowboys. She's not like that. The best ones aren't."

It was refreshing to hear her speak this way, because over the years I had endured some negative interactions with various members of various police forces, and while I concede that this was usually as a result of some justifiable investigation into my violent behavior, it still felt good to hear it.

"You must be very proud of her," I said.

"I sure am," she said, and I could tell she really meant it by the way a smile came onto her face.

"I do not believe that we appreciate police officers enough for what they do to keep our society safe."

"Shelley would be the first to agree with you. But every now and again, someone will walk up to her and say, 'Thank you for your service.' That's all an officer needs to hear every once in a while: 'Thank you for your service.' And she says that whatever doubts she has about the job go melting away."

This was a phrase commonly said to military veterans, but then I figured it should apply equally to police officers and fire officers and all other civil servants who put their lives in danger every day, or simply do good, honest work for the betterment of society.

Just then, the jury attendant came into the room and said that the trial was set to begin, so one by one we all filed out of the room, myself included, but not before I handed the jury attendant a small, folded, piece of paper that I had prepared that morning after breakfast.

As I did, I said, "Thank you for your service," and while I couldn't say that all his doubts went melting away, assuming he even had any, a small smile did curl up onto his face, and in that moment I knew that I already liked Shelley and her sister.

Chapter 7

One of the rules that the judge had given us yesterday was that if we had any questions throughout the proceedings that we should write them down on a small slip of paper without identifying ourselves and then hand it to our assigned jury attendant. That person would then bring the question into the courtroom and provide it to the judge, who would discuss it with the lawyers and choose best how to answer.

"I have a note from one of the jurors," said the judge, flatly, after we'd all been seated. Then she turned to us and said, "While we would normally excuse the jury while we considered the question, I believe that due to the nature of the question I can simply read it aloud with everyone present."

I noticed that the lawyers looked somewhat perplexed by this. Then the judge read my note aloud: "What is the dog's name?"

I saw some of the people smile after she said it, and I also saw a few of the jurors looking around, and the retired police officer let out a loud, "harrumph," as if maybe the question was stupid, even though I knew that it wasn't. Then the judge asked the lawyers if they had any issue with answering the question, and after nobody seemed to have a problem with it, the prosecutor told us that the dog's name was Herbert.

Then the judge turned to face us, only it seemed as if she was mostly looking at me.

"Ladies and gentlemen, this is going to be a long trial, and I hope that most of your questions will be answered as the matter proceeds. However, I would ask that you refrain from asking questions about the evidence. Please just listen to the evidence that is presented in court and base your deliberations on what you hear." Then she paused, before adding, rather sternly, "And of course we do not wish to extend or make light of these proceedings."

Again I felt that she was looking at me when she said it, and I felt that perhaps I had given myself away somehow, or perhaps the court registrar had told her who'd provided the note. Either way, I did my best not to betray an emotional reaction, which came rather easily to me, and after a few moments she invited the prosecutor to call her first witness.

Just before the prosecutor stood up to make her way to the podium, I noticed another person staring at me, only this person was seated in the courtroom. It was the English detective who'd been investigating me for the disappearance of my neighbor's boyfriend. When we had first entered the courtroom, I'd seen him approach her, and they had a terse discussion while he'd been pointing in my direction, only the prosecutor had just held out her hands as if to say, "What do you want me to do about it?"

I can only imagine that he was protesting my inclusion on the jury, but I suspect there was nothing the prosecutor could do about it. Now he was staring at me rather intently from a few rows back.

"I call Billy Baker to the stand," declared the prosecutor.

We'd all been given pads of paper and pens to make notes, so I jotted down the name of the first witness just as a man of about thirty wearing a blue suit walked up and stepped into the witness box. He swore an oath on the bible to tell the truth.

"Mr. Baker," said the prosecutor, "please tell us how you knew Shirley Baker."

"She was my wife," he said.

"How long were you married?"

"Two years," he said. "We had been together for five."

"And where did you live?"

"We lived at 42 Hancock Lane."

I noted this, too, as I felt it might be important.

"This is a house?"

"Yes."

"Is this the house?" she asked, approaching with a photograph.

"It is."

"First exhibit," she said, handing it up to the court.

EXHIBIT #1 – Photograph of House: 42 Hancock Lane.

"And how would you describe your relationship with your wife?"

"It was wonderful," he said, raising a handkerchief to his eyes for the first time. "She was the love of my life."

I noticed Shelley's sister's eyes had welled up, as had the eyes of a few others.

"Any issues between you?"

"There was an incident a few years ago when we had both had a little too much to drink, and police were called. It was just a misunderstanding."

"Any charges?"

"None," he said. "Like I said, it was a misunder-standing. I was more embarrassed than anything."

"Any children?"

"We hadn't tried yet."

"So you lived alone?"

"Just with the dog," he said.

The prosecutor then asked Mr. Baker to, "please tell us about the day of 'the incident'," which was a euphemism for cold-blooded murder, and one that I had sometimes even used in my own mind when reflecting on some of the crimes I had committed. People often used euphemisms to describe unpleasant things, like calling someone "big-boned" instead of fat, or writing that someone, "passed away suddenly" in an obituary rather than saying the person was ripped apart and eaten by a black bear. And even if this particular euphemism lacked precision, it was likely a better way to introduce the subject matter than by asking Mr. Baker to, "tell us about the day your wife was brutally bludgeoned to death with a marble bookend."

"I work for a company that sells and services copy machines," he said. "It was a workday, so the hours depend on the meetings we have scheduled and the type of work that comes up. That day I had to work late because I was meeting with a new client trying to close a sale and service contract for twenty copiers. The meeting didn't end until eight, and I didn't get home until close to nine."

"Take us through what happened next, when you got home."

"I parked in the driveway like I usually do and went in through the front door."

"And what happened next?"

"I immediately knew something was wrong because the front door was unlocked, and it was never unlocked."

"And what happened next?" she said, which seemed to be something she liked to say.

"As soon as I got inside, I could see that our place had been ransacked. Items were knocked over or missing. I called out Shirley's name, but there was no answer. That's when I started to panic, so I ran upstairs, and that's when I found her…"

Mr. Baker's voice trailed off and he started crying. Then he managed to say, through more sobs, that he'd found his wife still and bloodied on the floor in the master bedroom, and that she wasn't breathing.

"I called nine-one-one right away, but it was too late."

The prosecutor took Mr. Baker through some additional evidence, to help focus some details. Then she asked him if he knew either of the two men seated at the defendant's table. Mr. Butler looked them both over and said that he did not, and that to the best of his knowledge neither did his wife, and that they would never have had a lawful basis to be inside their home. These seemed like rather innocuous questions, only I would soon learn that they weren't as innocuous as I thought.

After she sat down, the judge invited the two defense counsels to begin their cross-examination, and Mr. Crooks's lawyer went first, apparently because Mr. Crooks's last name came in the alphabet before Mr. Munroe's.

Just as he had done yesterday, Mr. Crooks's attorney was rather forceful in the way he conducted himself. As soon as he stood up, he moved quickly to the lectern and challenged Mr. Baker's claim that he and his wife were on good terms, citing the domestic incident report that had previously been mentioned.

"A misunderstanding, is that what you called it?" Only he said it in a mocking fashion.

"Yes," said Mr. Baker.

"Sir, would you be surprised to hear that I have a copy of that report right here in my hand?" and he thrust a piece of paper high into the air when he said it. I had often seen such demonstrative antics from watching various court dramas on television. Lawyers often used them when they felt their case was weak, so as to artificially heighten the effect of that particular piece of evidence or submission. In fact, it was entirely possible that he wasn't even holding a police report at all, but had just scribbled down what he might like for lunch. This sort of thing was referred to as a "parlor trick" – which was to say that they were games or shenanigans that lawyers would play in order to trick the witnesses or even to distract the jury from what was important.

Mr. Baker seemed taken aback by this, and although the prosecutor stood up and objected, the judge allowed the questioning to continue.

"I haven't seen that," said Mr. Baker.

"That is not what I asked," said the lawyer, "Mr. Baker, did you have trouble understanding my question, or do you just not want to answer it?"

Mr. Baker seemed annoyed with either the question or the tone or both, and it appeared that he might even be angry by how he was now clenching the handkerchief.

"It would not surprise me if you had a report," he said.

"All right then," said Mr. Crooks' lawyer. "And now I'm going to give you a chance to come clean. You know, about what happened three years ago. I'm going to give you a chance to come clean and tell it straight."

"Is there a question in there somewhere?" asked Mr. Baker, and he indeed seemed angry now as I could see his face becoming red.

"My question, sir, is do you maintain that it was a simple misunderstanding, what happened between you and your wife?" He turned to the jury and smirked as he asked the question.

I saw Mr. Baker fidget some in his seat before answering.

"I do," he said, and he said it rather defiantly.

"Well then, let me read from this report, and let's see if we can figure this out together."

Again the prosecutor rose to object, but again she was overruled. That was when Mr. Crooks's lawyer started reading from the paper in his hands. As it turned out he actually did have the police report, and while I still felt his behavior to be unprofessional, he at least seemed to be resourceful.

"Ms. Shirley Glavine," then he paused, before saying, "That was your wife's maiden name, is that right, sir?"

He nodded in the witness box as he said, "Yes," but it wasn't a friendly nod.

"Ms. Shirley Glavine," continued the lawyer, reading from the paper, "phoned 911 to report that she had just been struck by her fiancée. She said that she had also been choked," he then paused again to look in our direction, before repeating the words, "just been choked," as if for added affect, before continuing.

"The police responded, where they found Ms. Glavine hiding, crying in the – now wait for it – in the master bathroom. She had a bruise on her eye and red marks around her neck."

I was watching Mr. Baker as the lawyer read this, and I could see his face growing redder and redder. Finally, he blurted out, "She admitted that she had lied about that," visibly frustrated. "She lied and there were no charges filed."

"So, she had an alternative version of the events, from the time she called 911 to the time of the police arrival ten minutes later, is that the case, Mr. Baker?"

"She told the truth," he said.

"And the marks on her face?" scoffed the lawyer.

"She admitted that she had attacked me and fallen over," he said. "It should all be there in that report," he said, pointing.

"How very convenient for you," said the lawyer.

"It's true," he said.

"Yes, well, if only we could ask your wife about it," responded the lawyer, rather condescendingly.

Mr. Baker jumped to his feet in the witness box and yelled out how he loved his wife as he was pointing angrily at Mr. Crooks's defense counsel, which was probably the type of reaction that the lawyer had been trying to goad him into all along. Then the judge banged her gavel down onto her dais shouting, "Adjourned!" and excused all of us for a short break to allow tempers to cool, and as we were all filing out of the courtroom, I could still see Mr. Baker's face glowing red.

Chapter 8

We were called back into the courtroom ten minutes later after order had been restored.

By then everyone was seated in a calm fashion, and I could see that Mr. Baker's skin color had mostly gone back to normal. Once we were all seated, the judge invited Mr. Crooks's defense lawyer to continue his cross-examination. He did so by suggesting that when the first police officer found Mr. Baker at the scene, he was overtop the victim apologizing profusely.

"You were saying 'I'm sorry' over and over, weren't you?"

"I don't remember what I was saying then, I was in shock."

"So then you don't deny it, apologizing to your dead wife."

"I can't deny something I don't remember."

This seemed a fair point, and I made a note of it.

"Do you remember why you might have said it, if you didn't feel that you were responsible?" asked the lawyer.

Again Mr. Baker's face went red, and it seemed as if he wanted to come out of his chair for a second time.

"Maybe because I was late coming home," he said. "Maybe I said it because I blamed myself for not being there."

Then Mr. Crooks' defense lawyer paused, leaning as far as he could over the lectern, "Or maybe it's because you lost your temper again like you did three years ago?"

At this suggestion Mr. Baker again jumped to his feet and began yelling at the lawyer, again forcing the judge to slam her gavel down multiple times to restore order. This time, however, she did not excuse us from the courtroom. She simply warned the parties that decorum was to be respected in her courtroom, and that the next person who fell out of line would be cited for contempt.

"No more questions," said the lawyer, again smirking at the jury before returning to his seat.

Mr. Munroe's counsel went next, only he did not ask many questions. He also took a much more professional approach than the previous lawyer, and he even started off by apologizing for Mr. Baker's loss. When he began his questioning, he pointed to his client and confirmed with Mr. Baker that he had surely never seen Mr. Munroe before, and that there was clearly no history of animus between Mr. Munroe and his wife, all of which Mr. Baker fairly conceded. He then said to Mr. Baker that if it wasn't him who'd harmed his wife, he surely did not see who it was who did, and Mr. Baker conceded that as well, just as he conceded that he could not tell if one or more people had been upstairs where he had located his wife. Then Mr. Munroe's lawyer apologized once more and sat down.

⌘

Following the conclusion of Mr. Baker's evidence, we broke for lunch. Once again we were brought back to our small jury room by the attendant, at which point he took orders for sandwiches from all of us and immediately set out to retrieve them.

We weren't alone long before I saw the retired police officer step to the center of the room.

He said, "So, at least we got the dog's name straight," only he said it in a mocking tone, and he was clearly alluding to my question from earlier that morning.

"Who was it, anyway, which one of you asked it?"

Then I saw him approach the young student. She had her earphones in and was reading her book, and it looked like she was now well past page 171.

"Was it you?"

I saw her pull down one of her earphones, and it went dangling from her side.

"What's that?"

"Just wanted to know if it was you asking about the dog this morning? I know how you kids are these days."

"What does that mean?" she said.

"Nothing," he said, throwing up his hands, "forget I said anything. This is a safe space, after all."

That was when I got up, told him to leave her alone, and said that it was me who'd asked the question.

"Well, why am I not surprised?" he said, and then he started laughing.

That was when Shelley's sister said, "Why don't you just fuck off?"

She said it under her breath, but apparently not far enough under it because juror number four must have heard it, and so he moved over to her and said, "What was that, what'd you say?"

She didn't respond. Instead she just turned her head down to her knees, which were bent up toward her chest, at which point he added, rather derisively, "Why don't you just stick to the pole, honey?"

I heard the CEO laugh when he said it, and one or two others. That's when I stepped forward and told him to leave her alone. Then he put his hands up at his side as if I had a gun on him, and he backed up as he did it, only he did it smiling, as if it were all a big joke. That was when the door opened and someone came in with some beverages, so everyone got quiet, and it wasn't long after that when the jury attendant came into the room wheeling in platters of sandwiches and cookies on a cart.

After that, we all ate our food without incident, and I ate too, even though I had mostly lost my appetite. This, of course, was yet another euphemism, because you couldn't actually lose your appetite like you could lose your keys or your wallet. And in my case it wasn't so much that my stomach wasn't hungry, so much as it was that I was preoccupied, which was itself just another euphemism for what I was really thinking, which was a strong desire to see juror number four as red and open.

Chapter 9

The evidence continued after lunch.

The next witness in the trial was the lead investigating police officer. She testified that she was the first officer on scene, and that she located Mr. Baker and his wife upstairs in the master bedroom, and that Mr. Baker was huddled over his wife crying and saying that he was sorry.

"I did not know what he meant by that," she said, "but I have responded to many crime scenes, and people say many unusual things when they are in shock."

"What did you do when you saw him like that?"

"I just asked him to step away from the body as this was a crime scene, and if we were to hope to catch the person who did this, that we needed to ensure the scene was not contaminated. I also wasn't certain if he'd been involved, so I wanted to ensure my own safety at that time, too."

"And what happened next?"

"I managed to calm him down, and then I seated him outside the room so he wouldn't have to see his wife that way."

"And what happened next?" she said, which again seemed to be something that she really liked to say.

"Two more units arrived, and then the forensic identification unit arrived shortly after that. I helped them seal off the area and take pictures of the deceased and the entire house."

The prosecutor walked forward and showed the officer a series of photographs, and after confirming that those were the photographs taken, they were entered as the next exhibit.

Exhibit #2 – Crime Scene Photos

"Did your team locate anything? Any prints or DNA?"

"We did not locate any prints upstairs, but we did discover a hair on the bedroom floor, just a few feet from the body, and we sent it to the lab for analysis."

"And what did you do next?"

"A number of items were stolen, so we flagged these on our computer, then kept watch on various Internet sites and checked with various pawnbrokers both inside and outside of town. About two weeks later, we received word from a pawnshop an hour outside of town that they had recently acquired a pair of brass candlesticks with a lion's head engraved on the base. That was the break we needed."

It would appear that these were distinctive candlesticks that were taken from the home during the burglary. This particular pawnshop had a surveillance video camera, so when they checked the footage, they determined that it was Mr. Munroe who'd sold the items, after which they obtained an arrest warrant.

"And after arresting Mr. Munroe, what did you do next?"

"We obtained his phone records, and that helped us to determine that Mr. Crooks was also involved, based on the calls and messages between the parties."

"And what happened next?"

"We had obtained a DNA warrant from a judge, and collected a bodily substance from Mr. Munroe. We then sent that sample to the same lab where we'd sent the hair that was found on the bedroom floor."

"And was it a match?"

"It was not, at least not to Mr. Munroe. However, when we did ultimately arrest Mr. Crooks, we also obtained a warrant for a sample of his DNA. And we sent that sample to the same lab."

The prosecutor walked forward with a multi-page document.

"Do you recognize this?"

"Yes, that is the report that came back from the lab."

"And what does it tell us?"

"It says that Mr. Crooks's DNA is a match to the hair we found in the bedroom, three feet from the body."

Exhibit #3 – DNA Report

"Can you tell us how Mrs. Baker was killed?"

"Blunt force trauma," she said. "With a marble bookend that was left behind at the scene."

The bookend, we were told, was normally kept above a mantle downstairs on the first floor.

"Was Mr. Butler ever a suspect in this case?" she asked, after returning to the podium.

"The spouse is always a suspect, but he was cleared."

"How so?"

"His alibi checked out."

"His alibi?"

"We contacted the person he claimed to have met with that night…a Mr. Ned Jarvis. And Mr. Jarvis confirms they had met at approximately the same time that night to discuss business."

After a few more questions, the prosecutor sat down and the defense lawyers had their turn. As expected, Mr. Crooks' defense lawyer was vocal and aggressive in his questioning. He suggested that the officer did not do enough to investigate Mr. Baker's alibi.

"The forensic pathologist says that she was dead at least two hours before Mr. Baker arrived home," said the officer.

"Yes," said the lawyer, his voice raised, "but what if she was dead already, as I expect you will hear from my client," and he pointed to Mr. Crooks, as he liked to do. "What if she had been killed just moments before Mr. Baker claims to have attended this business meeting."

"The time frame we had from the doctor, he would have had to come home from work, murder her, and be in his car only seconds later, make perfect time to the appointment, and conduct the business meeting as if nothing had happened."

"But it is possible?" yelled the lawyer, throwing his hands up.

"It is highly unlikely," said the officer, at which point the lawyer repeated his last question, even louder.

Then the judge banged her gavel and said, "asked and answered," and the defense lawyer moved on, only he was grinning as he did.

By the end of the day, both counsels had cross-examined the police officer. Then, given the lateness of the day, the judge decided that we would pick up with the next witness tomorrow morning.

"Adjourned," she called, before banging loudly with her gavel, which was something that she seemed to enjoy.

Whether it was breaking for lunch, or for the lawyers to speak, or even when stopping for the day, she would always loudly pronounce an adjournment with a smack of her gavel, and as it turns out, this time was no different.

Chapter 10

Over the next several days we heard from a number of other witnesses, and I did my best to take notes even though I was still sick and getting sicker. I made bullet points of what I thought were key pieces of evidence:

It had not been easy to identify Mr. Munroe from the video footage at the pawnshop, but finally a police officer recognized him from an old arrest, and that is how they were able to identify him.

After arresting Mr. Munroe, they obtained a search warrant for his telephone, and it showed many phone calls and messages with Mr. Crooks, suggesting some level of planning a theft. This was how they were able to identify Mr. Crooks as his co-conspirator.

That use of something called "triangulation" showed that Mr. Munroe's cell phone was pinging against the cellular telephone tower nearest to the Baker household during the time of the offence.

A video of Mr. Munroe's interview was played, where he cried and said that they never went there to hurt anyone, and that they just went to steal. He admitted that he and Mr. Crooks planned the burglary, but said that he never went upstairs where Mrs. Baker was found.

Mr. Munroe's fingerprints were apparently found on the doorknob where the dog had been locked up. The dog was beaten and bloodied. It made me angry to hear it, and I felt myself squeezing my pen much more tightly than I had before. I'd even looked over at Mr. Munroe as the details came out, and I watched as he bent his head down.

The prosecution closed its case just after four o'clock on Friday, and the judge had apparently had enough, because she suddenly slammed her gavel down and said, "Adjourned," without warning, and so we were all sent home until Monday morning with strict orders not to discuss the evidence with anyone, and while I was anxious to hear from the accused parties, I was just as happy to have a break, especially from juror number four, who continued to conduct himself in a rather loud and boorish manner.

I walked outside with Shelley's sister, who I had gotten to know better throughout the week, and she asked me if I had any plans for the weekend.

"I'm staying with my friend Gordon," I said. "I thought that I might go home and visit my son and my dog."

She got a sad look on her face when I said it. "Things not going well at home?"

"Donna is upset with me."

"That your wife?"

"She is my son's mother," I said. I said it because it was true.

Suddenly, she got very quiet, then smiled as she turned her head down, and I think I might have even called it a shy smile.

"Look, I'm not really supposed to do this, but you seem like a nice guy and all. I'm going to be working at The Rocksteady tonight if you're lonely. I mean, if it wouldn't be weird."

I wasn't sure if I should go, not only because my sore throat had gotten worse throughout the week and I was starting to feel feverish, but, given that I was in a committed relationship, I considered whether watching naked women might qualify as some form of visual adultery. Only then Shelley's sister became rather flustered and embarrassed and she said she only meant it as friends, and I felt as if I might have offended her by taking so long to respond, so I said that I might stop by sometime this weekend if there was time, which was an easy commitment to make, since I figured there probably wouldn't be.

After I said it, she got a big smile on her face and then she said, "Well, til then, adjourned," and she laughed and made a motion in the air like she was striking a gavel.

I watched as she walked away and couldn't help think about how attractive she was, and how much I liked her for standing up to juror number four. That was when I heard a voice from the side.

"Well, look what we've got here, my good friend Sonny Jim. That's who that is, that's Sonny Jim all right if I've ever seen him!"

I turned around to see the English detective walking up the courthouse steps. He must have been waiting for court to conclude so that he could intercept me.

"You don't look like a bloke too happy to see me, eh mate? Saw your face turn down as soon as you got a butcher of this old bobbie."

I hardly understood a word of what he said, but I guessed that he was saying I wasn't happy to see him.

"Hello," I said, because I didn't feel like saying anything more.

"Well, hello to you too, mate. Rough thing, this jury business, what with it being a murder and all. You feel up for it, mate?"

"I am legally obligated to attend."

"Yes, you are, quite right, right as ever, eh Sonny Jim?"

He liked to call me that even though it wasn't actually my name.

"What do you want from me?"

"Want?" he asked, as if he were genuinely surprised. "What a curious question, a curious question indeed. What makes you think I want anything from you at all? Can't a bobbie come by and say hello to a good mate serving some good jury duty? And that's what you are, ain't you mate, a good mate doing his good civic duty?"

"I do not believe you are truly happy to see me," I said.

"No?"

"No."

"And why's that?"

"Because the last time we met, you seemed very angry with me."

"Water under the bridge, mate. Just caught me off guard is all, in that moment. Can't blame an old bobbie for being caught off guard, can you?"

"I suppose not."

"Of course not, old chap, cause you're a mate that gets the ways things are, aren't you mate? There's a good reasonable mate, not blaming an old bobbie."

"What do you want?" I said, only before he could answer I started to cough.

"You got a cold, mate?"

"I believe I am sick."

"Well, best get home then, and crack into the ginger. That's what the missus always tells me, when I'm feeling knackered—crack into the ginger. The friend you're staying with, maybe he's got some for you, or his lovely wife?"

This was the detective's way of telling me that he'd been watching me.

"I believe I should get home now."

I started walking away, and the detective didn't follow me.

"You know, we still haven't heard a peep," he called out, "from the Josh fella."

He was referring to my neighbor's boyfriend, who had recently gone missing.

"Why are you telling me?" I asked, even though I already knew that he suspected me.

"Oh, just thought you might want to know, a good mate like you, doing his good civic duty. That's what you are, of course, a good mate doing good civic duty."

I didn't say anything else. I just kept walking to my car, got inside, and pulled out of the parking space and onto the road.

The detective stepped out as I did, and he even took a few steps in my direction, where I saw him watching me through the rear-view mirror as I drove away.

Chapter 11

By the time I arrived at Gordon's, I was coughing rather dramatically. I'd even stopped off at a variety store to purchase some cough drops, but I was still coughing so much during dinner that Gordon told me I was going to "cough out a lung."

I managed to eat some food but I wasn't very hungry, so I left most of it on my plate. Then one of Gordon's children asked me if I was ok, and when I tried to say yes, I only ended up coughing again. That was when Sharon stood up and said that she was going to make me a cup of tea just like she'd done the past few nights. Gordon also got up from the table. He immediately went upstairs and returned with a bottle of red liquid.

"Here," he said, thrusting it out in front of me.

"What is it?"

"It's the hair of the dog that bit you. What the hell do you think it is? It's cough medicine."

The girls laughed when he said it, except then Sharon called out, "Gordon!" in a sharp tone, and then everyone got quiet.

"Try it," he said, after a moment. "Just don't take too much or you won't wake up. This is extra strength black market shit."

I couldn't tell if Gordon was joking or not, only it seemed like he wasn't.

Sharon came back with the tea a minute later.

"You drink this and then take a hot shower. You'll feel better."

I excused myself from the table, as my parents had taught me was good manners, and then I made my way downstairs with both the cup of tea and the bottle of cough syrup. I decided against calling home tonight because I wasn't feeling well and I thought it would be best to just get a good night's sleep, so I drank the tea and some of the cough syrup, then went to sleep right in my regular clothes because I was just so tired.

Only I was coughing too hard to stay asleep, so after a while I got up and consumed two more portions of Gordon's medicine. Then I tried to sleep again, only I tossed and turned for over an hour, and then finally I must have decided to go out, because that's what I did.

At first, I just drove around, but finally I ended up at The Rocksteady. I probably shouldn't have been driving, what with all the cough syrup I'd consumed and how I didn't even remember how I got there, but then I figured what was done was done and there was no sense beating myself up over it.

I walked up to the door and was stopped by a bouncer. He didn't ask me for any identification or anything. In fact he didn't say anything to me at all. He just looked me up and down and I did the same to him, and after going back and forth like that for longer than was comfortable, I stepped unmolested into the club.

The music was much louder inside, so I found a table away from the speakers, but still close enough so I could see the stage. There were two dancers on the stage, and neither was wearing any clothing but underwear.

I had only been to such an establishment once before when I was in college, but I hadn't much enjoyed how loud and smoky it was, or some of the things that were going on around me, so I never went back.

"Drink, sir?"

The server was only wearing a bra and a thong, but she also had on bunny ears and a tail. I had a rabbit when I was young, and I thought about asking her if she was able to pick her uniform, and if rabbits were her favorite animal, only then I thought that she might just have to wear whatever they give her, and that by highlighting her lack of autonomy on the issue, it might cause her to fall into some sort of malaise.

"Sir?"

I quickly ordered a beer because I realize I'd been making her wait, only then I realized how much cough syrup I'd already consumed and how maybe I shouldn't have added more alcohol to it, but she was already walking away, with her bunny tail wiggling behind her, so I figured it was too late to do anything about it.

That was when the music changed, and the two girls left the stage as a new song came on as a new girl stepped up. She was wearing red lingerie on her body and had a mask on her face that had some feathers on it. Then I started thinking about how her face was part of her body, too, and I wondered why I'd separated them in my thoughts as if they were two separate entities, though I suppose maybe my mind just sometimes liked being more specific about things, and as I was thinking about how specific I was being the woman removed her mask from her face which was also a part of her body, and I saw that it was Shelley's sister.

She moved slowly to one of the poles and twirled around it rather gracefully. Then she walked over to the front row where some young men were waving bills into the air, and she began to gyrate overtop of them. In this way she was similar to my dog Molly, who would also gyrate at my feet whenever I came home, only unlike Shelley's sister, Molly never needed outstretch bills to prompt her to do so.

The young men tucked the bills into her underwear, then she blew them a kiss and went back to the pole. I could see she was about to remove her top, when she finally noticed me seated in the crowd. I knew that she saw me because a smile curled up on her lips, and she stared intently in my direction as she removed her top, biting her bottom lip at the end. Then she turned away and twirled her top in the air several times before finally throwing it to the young men in the front row.

The waitress had delivered my beer halfway through her routine, and I had just taken a sip when Shelley's sister circled back closer to where I was. Then she bent over and removed her underwear, and when she straightened back up, she walked over to the pole where she twirled around a few times before throwing her underwear in my direction.

I had been thinking of Donna intermittently throughout this performance, as it occurred to me that she might not approve of what I was doing in that moment. But then she had asked me to leave and I figured that this was pretty much a separation, and even if that's not exactly what it was, I convinced myself of it as best I could. And while it might have just been a coincidence, this convincing became stronger each time Shelley's sister removed an article of clothing.

Once the song ended, she walked off the stage through some fog, and another woman took her place. Only I didn't want to see another woman. I wanted to see Shelley's sister. And as I was thinking about how much I wanted to see her, suddenly she appeared at my side and joined me in my booth.

"Well, hello there."

"Hello," I said, before taking another sip of my beer.

"I didn't think you'd come."

I asked her why she thought so, and she told me that I just hadn't seem very interested when she'd suggested it on the steps.

"But I'm glad you're here," she added.

She was wearing clothes again, but they were still rather provocative, and I could see most of her bosom, if people even still called it that.

"Will you get in trouble being here at my table?" I asked.

"They let me do what I want when it's not my turn."

"I see."

"Sometimes I'll do some dances for people, to earn some extra money."

"I would not want to see you lose money on my account."

"It's ok."

Only I didn't think it was ok, so I took out twenty dollars and gave it to her, and said that I would like her to have it as she sat there with me. She smiled when I did it, reaching out to collect it from the table. Only then, when the next song came on, she got up on her knees and straddled me where I was seated.

I tried to say something but she just held her finger to my lips. Then she removed her top and pulled my hands up to her breasts, and in that moment I couldn't help but be grateful that college was so expensive.

"I like how you stood up for that girl today."

I didn't respond because I was preoccupied. Only then she leaned in closer.

"I'm so proud of how you stood up to him."

She whispered it in my ear and then playfully bit the lobe as my hands caressed her. Then I felt her hand move down over my jeans and I began to swell in that general vicinity. I moved in to kiss her but she told me I couldn't, only then she whispered that I should meet her by dressing room three in five minutes, pointing at the back, and then she quickly got up and left.

I had just enough time to flag down the waitress with the bunny costume and pay for my beer, which I quickly gulped down. Then I went back the way she'd pointed. I had only just arrived to a set of doors when one opened and I was pulled inside.

It was dark, but I knew it was her based on how she smelled and how she tasted. She helped me to achieve it twice before she told me she had to go back out for another dance. She said that she shouldn't be more than twenty minutes, but I departed before she took the stage, and I didn't even say goodbye.

Chapter 12

Since I was already downtown, I decided to go for a walk, only it was colder than I thought it'd be, so I soon stopped into a pub for another beer and to get in from the cold.

I found a dark booth where I could order another beer and think about the events that had just transpired. That's when I thought of Donna again, and if she would have disapproved of me attending an establishment like that, I could only imagine how much she would have disapproved of what I had just done in dressing room number three.

I was only just starting to get down on myself for my questionable fidelity when I heard a familiar voice. It was coming from two tables over, where six men were crowded around two small tables that had been pushed together. I knew the voice sounded familiar, but it wasn't until I saw him that I realized it was juror number four.

When the waitress came to my table, I ordered another beer, then I slunk down toward the back of the booth to better conceal myself so I wouldn't be noticed.

Juror number four was talking loudly just like he did in the jury room, and he was laughing hard with the other men as they shared pitchers of beer, and since they were so loud I could overhear most of their conversation. Mostly they were talking about the president, and while several of them mentioned "stupid immigrants," it seemed that no one at the table was all that interested in speaking about the intelligent ones.

That was when I heard one of the older men ask him about the case. I figured he wasn't going to answer, since we'd been instructed by the judge not to discuss it with anyone, only he answered without hesitation.

"Couple of thugs murdered some chick in a break-in."

It was clear that he'd already made up his mind about their guilt, which was another thing we weren't supposed to do. That's when one of the younger men at the table asked him if he thought the verdict would be unanimous.

"Hard to tell," he said. "Got some real pussies on this jury. An emu kid, a weirdo, and a whore."

I took another sip of my beer after he said this, only I was holding the glass so tightly I saw that my fingertips were going white, and I could already feel my breathing becoming more shallow with every passing moment.

He went on at some length about the case, and it seemed like some of the men weren't entirely comfortable with the conversation because while, some of them nodded and smiled, they were weak nods and smiles.

When the waitress finally came back to my table, I ordered another beer. Then I drank it slowly as I watched them share more pitchers of beer and say more things I didn't agree with. Then slowly, one by one, most of the other men started to leave, and by the end of the hour juror number four was seated with only one other person. I could hear him trying to convince his friend to accompany him to a "dive bar" just down the road, and soon enough he was successful, because they settled up and started for the door, so I deposited some money on the table and followed them outside from a safe distance.

I'd only stepped outside when I saw them stumbling to an old Buick across the road. Juror number four got into the driver's seat while the other man got into the passenger seat. Then they pulled out into the street, nearly hitting the car parked in front of them, and started down the road.

I followed in the direction they'd gone, only I was on foot, and rather stumbly, so I watched as the car drew further and further away. Then I saw the brake lights come on, and then the car seemed to disappear.

I made my way to where I'd lost sight of it, which was six blocks ahead. Then I spotted the vehicle on one of the side streets, where it was parked crooked against the curb. It was parked in front of a grungy looking building with a neon sign that said "Beer" on it, so I figured that was where they must have gone, so I went inside.

It wasn't much of a dive bar. It was dark and heavy with cigarette smoke, even though smoking had been banned in public establishments some time ago. I soon noticed them seated at the bar, so I found a spot at a table where I could watch them from a safe distance. It was harder to blend in at this second bar because there were hardly any people there, but since it was so dark and smoky that seemed to help, and I don't believe he noticed me.

By then my scary thoughts had started to subside, only then I saw him laughing, and just hearing his voice and seeing the look on his face made so angry, and I started thinking about the things he'd said to the student, and to Shelley's sister, and then I started hearing her words in my head.

I like how you stood up for that girl today.

Still laughing.

I'm so proud of how you stood up to him.

I couldn't hear the words he was saying, but I watched his mouth moving up and down, and I just knew that whatever he was saying was despicable. That was when he slid off his stool and made his way toward the restrooms, and so I followed him rather mechanically.

By the time I went in, he'd pulled up to a urinal. He was swaying as he stood, and it seemed like he might even lose his balance and fall all the way over, only he didn't. There was nobody in there but us because I'd already scanned for other people when I entered.

After zipping up he turned around to see me standing there. At first, he didn't seem to recognize me, only then I saw the slow recognition form, and he said, "Oh, you." He said it in a mean way, and I watched as his face bent into a sneer.

When I didn't respond, he said, "What are you, a fucking weirdo or something?" Only I still didn't respond. Instead, I kept hearing Shelley's sister say how proud of me she was, over and over and over in my mind, and then finally I told him that he needed to apologize to her.

"Apologize? To who?"

He was slurring his words, and I felt like he might not actually know who I was talking about, so I explained it to him. Only then he laughed.

"You think I ought to apologize, eh?"

"Yes," I said.

"And what should I say, exactly?"

"That is your decision," I said.

He grew quiet then, and he seemed to be thinking about it sincerely, only then I watched as he unzipped his pants again, and after pulling it out, he said "You think if I apologize I might get a freebie?" and my thoughts went wild, and then he said, "or maybe this is more to your liking?" and then he started laughing again real loud, only by then I could barely hear him because my mind was screaming so loud that his voice had gone away somewhere into the background, and as he laughed with his head back and his penis flapped out, I struck out my clenched fist without thinking, and I think I must have crushed his windpipe because he immediately fell to the ground gasping and squirming.

I thought that maybe I should run out and ask someone to call an ambulance, only instead of doing that I started kicking him in the head and face, which seemed like a rather contradictory action to what I had been just contemplating, but it all happened so fast, and there was really no time to dwell on the contradiction until later.

Once he stopped moving I fell back a few steps, and it finally registered what I'd done, so I fled outside and ran toward my vehicle, only I was so out of sorts that the run seemed to take forever, and I had only just gotten inside my car when I heard the sirens blazing in the distance, and that's when the world started to tilt left and right and back left again, and then the next thing everything went black.

Chapter 13

I woke up back in my bed still wearing my same clothes, which were now all wrinkly.

My body was stiff and sore, and my head was foggy, and I couldn't even recall how I got there. I rose as quickly as I could to check my body for any evidence, but there was none. No blood. No torn clothes. Only some sore muscles.

I managed to get to my feet, then I stumbled into the bathroom where I flipped on the light and checked myself over once more in the mirror. Everything seemed ok, but I disrobed just to be safe, and immediately took a shower. Then, after getting dressed, I went upstairs to find Gordon seated at the kitchen table with a newspaper in his hand. He had a special monocle that he could put up to one of his eyes and if he did that he could still read some.

"How'd you sleep?"

I didn't want to answer, for fear that I might incriminate myself, so I didn't say anything and just sat down.

"That good, eh?"

The front page was facing me, so I briefly scanned it for any news of a murder, but there was nothing. That was when I noticed Sharon in the kitchen.

"You want some breakfast?" she asked, and I nodded in her direction.

"I heard lots of moving around," said Gordon. "You get up and go for a walk or something?"

"Not that I remember," I said.

Normally, I tried to lie to people as little as possible, but in this instance it seemed to be unavoidable. Then I asked Gordon if I could have the newspaper when he was finished with it, and he said he was already done and immediately handed it over. I flipped through it quickly but didn't find anything in there about a murdered policeman. Only then I thought that it was possible he hadn't died at all, and maybe he was in intensive care. But whichever the case, I wondered if I'd be arrested and clapped into irons the moment I arrived back for jury duty, and just as I was thinking of all that, I started coughing again.

"Damn, you still got it?" said Gordon.

Sharon brought me a plate with some eggs and toast, and a hot cup of tea. I quickly consumed everything and felt better after I did.

"We're going bowling today if you'd like to come," said Sharon.

"I believe I should visit Donna and Toby," I said.

"She gonna let you come home, or what?" said Gordon. Then Sharon called out Gordon's name as if she was mortified by what he'd just said.

"What? It's been two weeks. She accused him of something he didn't do!"

"Perhaps she will feel differently today," I said, but Gordon just shook his head with a look of frustration. I knew that Gordon felt that I was the victim in all of this. However, I couldn't help thinking about Shelley's sister and what we'd done in dressing room number three, and even if Donna was technically mistaken about her accusation when she'd first levied it, I wondered if maybe she was right after all, only her accusation was misplaced in time.

"Well, we just hope it works out well for you both," said Sharon, who was not only a clean person and a good person, but also a supportive one.

I thanked them both for all they had done for me, then quickly went out to my car, checking the seat and the steering wheel to ensure there was no blood before I finally started toward home.

By then I was thinking about a book I'd been forced to read in high school, and while I didn't much appreciate it back then, it resonated with me much more in that moment. It was a story about a sailor by Herman Melville, and I remember how the sailor committed murder by striking out at his commanding officer, and how this made him a tragic figure because he was actually the good guy and had just lashed out involuntarily as a result of being bullied. And while I couldn't help think that my own situation was very much like that one, I did have to concede that the extra six kicks I'd delivered to his head after he'd hit the ground might have slightly distinguished our cases.

Chapter 14

Ipulled into my driveway twenty minutes later.

I'd listened to the local news station all the way over, but there was nothing about the attack of a former police officer. Still, I couldn't help thinking about what evidence might link me to the crime. I hadn't yet ordered a beer, so they shouldn't have my fingerprints on anything, and I figured that a place like that might not even have any cameras, so I started thinking that there might not be anything that could identify me at all, aside from juror number four himself, if he'd even survived.

"Well, are you going to come inside or what?"

I had been standing outside my car thinking of all this when Donna's voice drew my attention. She was standing at the top of the driveway before she turned back for the door, and I followed her inside.

I had barely stepped into the foyer before Molly came bounding my way, jumping into the air and barking and generally carrying on in an irresponsible manner.

"Where's Toby?"

"He's taking a nap," she said. "We were up early to go swimming."

Given all that had recently transpired, I'd forgotten that Toby had swimming lessons on Saturday morning. He was only four and half years old, but we were encouraged to get him swimming earlier than later, otherwise he might be afraid of the water. When I'd first heard this I thought it was silly that anyone would be scared of water, only then I remembered how people were scared of all sorts of innocuous things, like airplanes and mirrors and democratic socialism, so I supposed it made sense that Toby might be scared of water if he were not exposed to it early.

Donna invited me into the living room, which I thought was strange since it was as much my house as it was hers, but I accepted the offer to be gracious and because I thought it would have been strange to turn it down simply on that basis. We then sat together on the couch, only with a couple of feet in-between us.

"I spoke to Hayley," she said softly.

"I see."

"Not even an hour after our last call. She came by to visit. She asked where you were because she hadn't seen you in a while."

"What did you tell her?"

"I told her the truth. I told her that I thought you may have been unfaithful."

"I see."

"You don't seem surprised?"

The fact was that I wasn't surprised. Not only because I had suggested she might do it, but because I knew that Donna was generally governed by her emotions and had difficulty not acting on her impulses, only I left those last parts off, because for whatever reason, she also didn't like being reminded of those things, no matter how true they were.

"Well, she was shocked when I suggested it. I mean, positively gobsmacked."

I stared straight ahead after she said it, so then after a moment, she added, "What are you thinking about?"

I was actually thinking about how I hadn't heard that last word in a really long time, and I thought about how powerful it was, and how it should probably be used more often. That was when I recognized that my reaction about her use of the word was actually the definition of the word itself, which was a curious happenstance, and I thought about how funny it was that things went like they did, and I briefly thought about discussing the coincidence with Donna, only instead I just asked, "How do you know she was surprised?" because my experience had taught me that people usually weren't as gobsmacked about these sorts of thoughts as I was.

"Just the look in her face. Her expression. The tone in her voice."

"And what happened next?"

I'd only just said it when I realized that I'd just said the same thing that the female prosecutor had been saying over and over during the trial, and I realized then why she had been repeating those words so often, because it was a simple way to prompt the witness forward and to uncover more information, and I couldn't help but laugh when I said it.

"What's so funny?" asked Donna.

I explained what it was, only she didn't find it nearly as funny as I did. This may have been because she was trying to explain something important and it may have appeared as if I was making light of the subject or not taking things seriously, which couldn't have been further from the truth. Only I had found in my life that sometimes thoughts would just jump to the forefront of my mind, and sometimes it was simply impossible to ignore them, and this turned out to be another one of those times.

"Anyway," she continued, "I thought about it some more, and I know you would never cheat on me. I mean, I just know that you wouldn't."

As soon as she said this, I again started thinking about Shelley's sister, and about what we'd done last night in dressing room number three, and I couldn't help but feel awful about it. Only then I allowed for the possibility that I hadn't been unfaithful at all, since we were on something of a break, so although I may have been unfaithful to her, I also allowed for the possibility that I wasn't all the way unfaithful, given the circumstances.

"Well, aren't you going to say anything?"

I thought about it for a moment as I looked down at Molly, who had her head cocked to the side, and I thought that I should come clean about the whole night, since this seemed to be a moment of heartfelt honesty, and it seemed like a good opportunity to begin the relationship anew, so I took a deep breath, and then I finally spoke.

"I have something to tell you," I said.

I saw her face go quizzical, and then I hesitated to say more, only I didn't hesitate for long.

"Last night, I achieved it twice with Shelley's sister in dressing room number three, and I believe that I may have involuntarily killed juror number four in a bathroom."

She seemed startled by what I'd just said, which was understandable in the circumstances.

"Only it is possible he did not die," I added, "but was merely grievously injured."

Still, she stared quietly back at me, and it seemed like her face was almost about to bend into one of sympathy and understanding, only then at the last moment it veered into histrionics, and she began to scream incomprehensibly and to beat me on my chest with clenched fists. Then Molly ran forward barking wildly in a way that betrayed the fact that she had ever been to obedience school, and moments after that Toby came running down the stairs and then into the room crying, "Mommy," and

"Daddy," while pulling along his security blanket, which was clearly failing to do its job.

The fact was that I had merely rehearsed all of this in my mind, which was something that I liked to do because then I was able to toggle through some of the likely reactions, and while I saw some brief upside to being completely open and honest at this critical juncture in our relationship, I believed that the reaction I had just envisioned was the most probable outcome, and even if she could see her way past the cold-blooded murder, I couldn't help thinking that if I truly confessed to Donna that I had achieved it with a non-family-oriented dancer that she wouldn't so much see that as a continuation of open and honest discourse as much as a sudden and unforgivable betrayal. So instead of telling her anything about last night's activities, instead I just said, "Does this mean I can come home?" which seemed like the safest option, and one significantly more likely to maintain the domestic harmony that we'd just re-established.

Donna just looked at me silently when I said it, only then her head started into a slow nod as I saw tears come into her eyes, and then she started smiling as she came forward and grabbed me into a big hug. And as she embraced me there on the couch, I couldn't help think about how quickly things could change in life, and how I'd just been living in Gordon's basement and been involved in an important murder case, yet not even a day later I'd probably killed someone and had been of uncertain fidelity to Donna, and how Monday I'd probably be clapped into irons, but until then I would enjoy this time with my partner and my son and my dog and to a lesser extent the cat, and how all things considered, I was gobsmacked that my weekend hadn't turned out half-bad.

Chapter 15

As soon as Toby woke up he must have heard my voice because he came running down the stairs yelling, "Daddy, Daddy, Daddy," which was a repetitive thing that he sometimes did, even though I don't believe I'd ever given Toby cause to believe my hearing was flawed.

I knelt down on the floor as he ran up to me and we hugged. It was only the third time that I'd seen him since I'd been asked to move out, and because of the trial it had been nearly a full week since my last visit. When I finally pulled back, I saw tears rolling down his cheeks.

"Why are you crying?" I asked, only he didn't answer.

Toby kept telling me to stay, so I said that I would, given the conversation that I'd just had with Donna.

"But I do have to go to Gordon's to pick up my things."

Then Toby started crying again and kept saying, "No, no," once again as if I hadn't heard the first, "No." Then Donna suggested that he go with me to collect my things, and I thought that was a good idea, so that's what we decided to do.

By the time we got back to Gordon's, they'd already left to go bowling, so we had the place to ourselves. I put Toby on the floor where there were some of the girls' toys, and he started playing with them as I turned on the local news. Once again I didn't see any news about the retired policeman, so it made me wonder if perhaps it hadn't been quite as bad as I'd imagined it, only then I thought back to the images in my head, and how he'd been gasping for breath, and how I'd kicked his nose mostly into his head, and other such visuals that it made a fast recovery seem improbable. But for whatever reason there was still no mention of it, and I couldn't tell if this made me more or less nervous about my situation.

After I'd collected my things, I wrote a thank-you note for Gordon and his family, which I left on the kitchen table. Then I took Toby for an ice cream cone and then we went home so I could unpack my things. We then spent that day together watching television and later we all had dinner together when Toby told me about what had been happening at school, and just like that, things were mostly back to normal, at least if I blocked out everything I'd done the night before, so that's what I did.

Unfortunately, Sunday was a much more difficult day, because no matter how hard I tried, I couldn't help thinking about what was awaiting me the next morning when I checked in to continue the murder trial of Mr. Crooks and Mr. Munroe. I also felt increasing guilt about what I'd done, because even though the retired policeman might have been a mean-spirited and unpleasant person, he hadn't actually harmed anyone, except with his words, so I knew that he didn't deserve what I'd done to him.

I kept watching the news most of the day, but there was still no mention of it, only I knew from watching movies and television that the police sometimes kept these things out of the media in order to keep their investigation a secret. I also thought about how the English detective had been following me around, and how maybe he'd seen what I'd done that night, or at least had tracked my movements, and how maybe he was just waiting for me to turn up Monday morning to arrest me, in order to make a big show of it. I then began to feel tremendous anxiety, and though I briefly pondered packing my things and running away, I knew that sort of thing would immediately cement my guilt, and I also knew it would be unfair to Donna and Toby and Molly, and to a lesser extent the cat.

I was also thinking of something that my father used to tell me when I was younger. He used to tell me that, "boys take excuses, men take consequences." What he meant by that was that only immature people run from the problems they create, whereas responsible adults accept responsibility and face things head on, which was all to say that if I ran from what I'd done to juror number four then I would be taking the immature, cowardly way out. So regardless of my apprehension, I finally resigned myself to just enjoy the day as best I could under the circumstances and to face whatever consequences would arise the next day.

That night I was unable to achieve it with Donna. I feel that this was probably because I was nervous over the possible murder, though I suppose it may also have been residual feelings of guilt for being of uncertain fidelity. But whatever the reason, I couldn't do the things that we normally did, and so finally she helped me to achieve it with her hand and told me that she loved me, and even though that made me feel better, it didn't make me feel all the way better.

Chapter 16

Monday morning, I got up extra early so I could take Molly on a nice long walk, and I told her that she was such a good girl even though she hadn't done anything exceptional that morning beyond merely existing. Then I dropped Toby off at school with Donna, before kissing her and driving to the courthouse.

I continued to feel an immense amount of guilt and apprehension, and while I had committed crimes in the past, and my brain wanted to think about them from time to time, they had never bothered me to the same degree as this one.

Given my concern over juror number four, I'd hardly thought about Shelley's sister, and it only struck me as I walked in and saw her seated at the table that she might have felt our encounter was more than just a one-night stand, and that perhaps she might have developed an emotional attachment and might even wish to begin a relationship, and want to come home with me, and how before long she might even want Toby to start calling her "Mom". I thought about all of this as I walked over to where she was and sat down.

"Hey," she said. She was smiling wide but she seemed a little uncomfortable.

"Good morning."

Neither of us spoke for a few seconds, until she did.

"Look, I'm sorry about, you know…I shouldn't have done that."

I was surprised to hear her say it so candidly.

"Yes," I said.

"So you agree?" she said. She seemed surprised, which I found unusual, given that it was she who brought it up in the first place.

"I don't think it was anyone's fault," I said. "At least, I don't think you have any reason to feel ashamed."

She smiled at me when I said it, only it was weak smile.

"I nearly told Donna," I added, "only then I decided not to."

"Seriously?"

"Yes," I said.

I watched as she bowed her head, and she seemed rather perplexed, so I thought back about what I'd just said, only that was when the jury attendant stepped inside the room and called out attention.

"Good morning everyone. I want to thank you for attending so promptly. Unfortunately, there has been a development, and we will not be able to start on time as planned. I will provide you an update as soon as I can," and then just like that he left the room.

I'd half-expected him to enter the room with a police officer, or perhaps several, and be immediately taken into custody, and perhaps placed under a hot lamp for questioning if that was something they still did.

"I wonder what all that's about," said Shelley's sister.

"I suspect it has something to do with juror number four not being here," I said. I felt comfortable saying it, because by simply observing that one of the jurors was missing didn't in and of itself betray any level of guilt on my part because anyone could have seen it. I had also started thinking that if nobody saw me leave the bar, and they had no cameras, that they might just consider it a random act of violence, given that it was a dive bar on a shady side street.

I had only just started thinking about how I might actually evade liability for the attack when I saw Shelley's sister raise her hand in the air, and she had her pinky out pointing behind me, so I turned around and that was when I saw juror number four standing speaking with the Adventurer, and I immediately felt funny all over, like maybe I was in a dream, or some strange alternate reality, and I quickly rose from my seat and drifted over to where they were talking. Whatever they'd been discussing, they stopped as I grew closer. Then they both turned to me, as if expecting me to speak, only I didn't. Instead I just surveyed juror number four for any sign of wound or injury, of which I saw none.

"Hey there, friend?" said the Adventurer, in his usual friendly manner.

"You are uninjured," I said, looking intently at juror number four.

"What's that, fella?"

Still, they just stared at me, as I looked closely at his nose and his throat. That's when I felt my arm gripped firmly, and I was drawn aside by Shelley's sister, who led me back to where we'd previously been seated.

"What the hell is wrong with you?"

That was the first moment it occurred to me that Friday night's activities might not have actually happened.

"I'm sorry, I'm not feeling myself."

"Yeah, no shit."

I still wasn't sure what was real or not, so I asked her the last thing she remembered that we talked about, before today, because I felt like that was a relatively safe question, only she seemed embarrassed and declined to answer. That was when the jury attendant returned to the room to advise us that all the lawyers had now arrived, and the trial could resume. We filed in one by one back into the courtroom and into the jury box, my eyes trained on the retired police officer, whose nose and throat were still in all the right places.

Chapter 17

Mr. Crooks was the first witness that day.

His lawyer proceeded in the same angry, mercurial fashion as he had the week before, as if all of this was a great bother, and his client had suffered a great injustice even being charged.

"Mr. Crooks," he began, "how old are you?"

"I'm thirty-one."

"Do you have a criminal record?"

"Sure do."

"Tell us about it."

"Oooh," he pursed out his lips some as he said it, "must have about a half dozen B&E's, a fraud or two."

"Property offences," said the lawyer, loudly emphasizing the first word as he turned toward all of us in the jury box.

"Yes."

"Any violence on your record?" he asked.

"Just got a peace bond once," he said.

"Tell us about it."

"My girl went nuts once, came at me swinging when she found out I'd gotten with her friend. I grabbed her to stop her from hitting me, and I was the one that got charged."

"So you don't deny cheating on her?"

To that, Mr. Crooks turned toward the jury with something of a smirk and said, "What can I say? I'm a dog."

"What's that," said the lawyer, "you're 'a dog' you say?"

"Yeah, man, I'm a dog. What can you do?"

"No allegations of beating up a woman, then?"

"Hell, no."

"Unlike Mrs. Baker's husband," added his lawyer, turning toward us with a smile.

The prosecutor flew to her feet the moment he said it and objected, which was sustained by the judge.

"You will keep your exposition to yourself, counselor."

Mr. Crooks' lawyer bowed to the judge and apologized, only it didn't seem like a sincere apology, because he still had some remnant of the smile on his face. Then he continued examining his client.

"No weapons offences?" he asked.

"None."

"No sexual assaults."

"None."

"No murders," and again he called out the last word rather defiantly as he turned toward the jury box.

"No way, man!"

I saw Mr. Baker seated in the gallery, and he was shaking his head as Mr. Crooks testified.

"Tell us about that night then," said the lawyer. "Tell us what really happened."

Again the prosecutor rose to her feet, but before she even opened her mouth, the judge had slammed her gavel down and again admonished Mr. Crooks' lawyer to watch his exposition, so he apologized again, only again he did not seem contrite.

Throughout this testimony, I had felt an overwhelming urge to look at juror number four, who was seated almost directly behind me. I'd managed to avoid it until that moment, but finally I turned around to look at him, and I saw him staring sternly back, so I faced back around and by then the examination had continued.

"I'd cased the joint a day before, just to make sure it was good. Went up around, checked out some windows and such. They looked loaded."

"Loaded?" asked the lawyer.

"Yeah, like, fancy cars. You could see fancy shit through the windows. Loaded."

"So you 'cased the joint'. What do you mean by that?"

"I mean that I checked it out, to see what kind of the security they got. Didn't seem like they got any."

"All right then, tell us about that night."

This seemed to give pause to Mr. Crooks for the first time, and he straightened up in the witness box.

"We got there, me 'n Weeps. Must've been round eight."

"Weeps?"

"Yeah, my co-pilot, dawg," and he motioned toward Mr. Munroe.

"Why do you call him Weeps?"

"Just what we call him."

"So you and Weeps did what, once you got there?"

"We saw a car come out of the garage. Mean tint. We kept outside for maybe twenty. Lights all off. No movement. Figured they was both out."

"What did you do then?"

"Weeps, he parked on the road, and I went up to the front door. Knew they didn't have any security system. So I just jimmied it and went right in."

"What was your intent at that moment?"

"Man, we was just going there to plunder."

"Plunder?" said the lawyer.

"Yeah, like pirates and shit."

"You will watch your language in my courtroom," demanded the judge as she smacked her gavel.

When Mr. Crooks got started again, he talked about how he'd brought in some pillowcases and started filling them with valuables. He said that he'd only just made it to the bedroom when he realized something was awry, only he didn't use the word awry so much as an expletive that need not need be repeated.

"I seen her sprawled out on the floor, and I figured we better bounce."

"Did you see her move?"

"No."

"Did you touch the body?"

"Fuck, no!"

Another smack of the gavel.

"So what did you do then?"

"Just grabbed some more sh…" then he stopped, glancing over to the judge, "grabbed some more stuff, then we got steppin."

"So, you didn't leave when you saw the woman?"

"Not right away."

"You saw a body on the floor, but kept stealing?"

"Stuff still worth money all the same. Me 'n Weems gotta eat."

I could hear the old woman saying, "tsk tsk," beside me.

"What did you do next?"

"Weems, he musta got bored, cause he come in then. So, we grabbed s'more stuff together and then we split."

"Did you tell him about the body?"

"Nah."

"Why not?"

"No point. We got what we come for."

"Mr. Crooks," said the lawyer, again very sternly, "did you kill that woman?"

"Fuck, no!"

"Adjourned!" screamed the judge, and down came the gavel.

As we funneled back into our jury room, the judge simultaneously stormed off the bench. And just before exiting the courtroom, I could already see Mr. Crooks being led in shackles back to the prisoner's box, and then I immediately thought about chocolate milk.

Chapter 18

Why I thought of chocolate milk in that precise moment was bizarre, and not something that I could explain, except to say that the brain thinks curious things when it's left alone, and I suppose I was mostly leaving mine alone in that moment since it didn't take much effort to walk from one room to the next.

Throughout Mr. Crooks' testimony I had done my best to take notes, but the fact was that I was still in some state of shock over discovering that I had not killed juror number four, and that perhaps the entire night had been in my mind, only I still couldn't be sure of it.

I had been wondering about how this could have happened, only just as quickly I remembered all the cough medicine that I had consumed, and how Gordon had warned me to only take a small amount, and how maybe that was the reason my thoughts had been so extreme and even tricked me into believing that certain events had actually happened. Still, it worried me how completely I had been fooled, and while my mind often thought out elaborate scenarios and hypotheticals, I could always tell those apart from real life. This was the first time where my imagining had been so powerful and my mind had tricked me so thoroughly that I had truly imagined what had happened to be true, and while it did concern me to a degree, I figured that I would still have to rely on my mind to go forward in life, and how if it really wanted to trick me that it would probably get the final say about it, so I figured there was no point getting too fussed about it.

I had also found some sense of relief in the revelation that I had not murdered juror number four as I thought I had, which I'd settled in my mind as being mostly involuntary. I had only just arrived by the water cooler when I heard a voice from behind.

"You got something to say to me, pal?"

It was juror number four, and while I hadn't actually wanted to discuss it, I felt it couldn't hurt to share what I'd been thinking, and why I had been behaving so peculiarly. Which is to say, more peculiarly than normal.

"Yes," I said, "I wish to apologize."

"For what?"

I went on to explain how I'd had a dream in which I had assaulted him, and possibly even killed him, and how I felt tremendous guilt about what I'd done, even if it was only done in my head and under the influence of strong medication, and that even though it was only done in my mind, how I still felt sufficient guilt such that I wanted to apologize.

He seemed rather bewildered by it all. I then asked him if he'd read the Melville book with the young sailor, only he looked at me queerly when I said it.

"Is this a joke?"

"No," I said.

"Think you're being pretty funny, eh pal?"

Again I said that I wasn't, only he didn't seem to believe me. Then he told me that if I ever wanted to "man up" in real life that he would be here to greet me, then he got a drink of water from the water cooler and immediately crushed the paper cup that he'd just drunk from, perhaps as a demonstration of his strength, before tossing it into the garbage can.

That was when I went back and sat beside Shelley's sister.

"Are you feeling all right?" she asked, reaching out and placing her hand on my arm as she did.

"I'm not sure," I said. I said it because it was true.

"I'm sure you could ask to be excused if you're sick."

That was the first time that I thought I might indeed still be sick, and that perhaps this was the reason why I was feeling so unsettled, and my mind was running off to places it didn't usually go, which was saying something, because it routinely went to a lot of different places.

"I would not want to disrupt the process," I said.

"Screw that. My sister, Shelley, she says that court gets adjourned for all different reasons all the time. If you're sick, you shouldn't have to be here."

I thought that maybe it would for the best, only I had mostly stopped coughing by then, so I figured there was probably no good reason to go home. Only then I thought about it some more, and I wondered if maybe my body wasn't so much sick as much as my mind was. Only, I knew the way things worked in life was that if people couldn't actually see that you were sick they presumed that you weren't. I had always found this to be an odd approach to wellness because ninety percent of a person was beneath their skin and hair and couldn't be seen, and it seemed rather unscientific and borderline absurd to presume that any sickness would manifest itself visibly on that outside ten percent. However, this was the way most people believed, and often if they couldn't see blood or bones or sweat from a fever, they would presume that you were faking the illness just to get out of doing something, or to avoid a penalty or a consequence. I'd read in a magazine that this was called malingering, and given that the trial judge already believed I wanted to be excused, I felt that this would only add to her suspicions, and she might wrongly conclude that I might myself be a malingerer, even though she couldn't see the other ninety percent of me.

"I do not believe the judge would allow me to leave," I said.

"I don't think that's her call."

I figured that it probably was her call, since she had the robes and the gavel, but I did appreciate her concern.

I was just about to ask her about Friday night, as I was still confused over what had been real memories and what had been fake cough syrup memories, when the jury attendant re-appeared at our door and said that court was ready to proceed, so I got up and filed back inside with all the rest, all one hundred percent of me.

Chapter 19

The judge was already seated at the dais with a stern look on her face, and everything else was very much as it was before we left, including Mr. Crooks seated in the witness box, and his lawyer standing at the lectern.

Once we'd all been seated, the judge began speaking.

"Ladies and gentlemen of the jury, I want to apologize for the language you were subjected to during the last session of testimony. I have spoken to the parties, and I have been assured that it will not happen again."

She raised her tone at the end while glaring toward Mr. Crooks, and then his counsel. Neither responded, as if they weren't particularly repentant, but the lawyer did finally nod, so I figured that might be the end of it.

"Those are all my questions," he said, before Mr. Munroe's lawyer stepped up to the podium to begin asking his own questions. He got Mr. Crooks to admit that Mr. Munroe was only the getaway driver, and that he only entered the home for a short period of time, and that he never went upstairs to the second floor where the body was. Upon receiving those concessions, the lawyer sat down.

The prosecutor then had her turn, and while she was able to cross-examine him about various elements of his story, the fact was that he had admitted to being in the home and stealing the items that were pawned, and even to being upstairs where his hair had been found, so there was not much gained from it. When pressed on his version of events, Mr. Crooks just repeatedly said that the woman appeared beat up but was already dead when he saw her.

The next witness was Mr. Munroe. He initially testified much the same way as Mr. Crooks had, in that they had targeted that particular house because it looked like they had a lot of money and valuables. Mr. Munroe stated that he stayed in the car for the first twenty minutes, and only went inside because he felt that it was taking too long.

"Did you finally go inside?" his lawyer asked.

"Yes."

"Why did you go inside?"

"Because we'd agreed it would be a quick job. Grab as much jewelry and electronics as possible in a bag and leave. We were supposed to be gone in ten minutes. So I went in to bring him out."

"What did you see when you went inside?"

"Not too much, it was mostly dark, and I didn't want to turn any lights on. That was when I heard the dog barking on the other side of the door."

"Which door?"

"I think it was from one of the downstairs doors. Like maybe a laundry room or something."

"Your fingerprint was on that door handle."

"Yeah, I was going to go in, but then I thought better of it."

"And then what happened?"

"I started going up the stairs, lookin for Crooksy, but as soon as I got halfway up, I seen him come out of one of the rooms with a bag of stuff."

"Did he have any sort of weapon in his hand? Anything that might be used as a weapon?"

"Nah, nah, nothin like that."

"Then what happened?"

Just like the prosecutor, this was something that Mr. Munroe's lawyer seemed to enjoy saying.

"Then I helped him grab s'more stuff from the ground floor since I was already inside, and then we split."

"Did you ever see the victim?"

"Nah, nah," he said, shaking his head.

"And then what happened?"

"We threw everything in the van, then I got back into the driver's seat, and Crooksy, he jumped in beside me and we got to steppin."

"Got to steppin?"

"I mean we got the hell out of there."

"And, Mr. Crooks, did you see any blood on him?"

"Nah, nah, nothing like that."

"Did he say anything to you?"

Up until this point, it appeared that Mr. Munroe might have been a helpful witness to Mr. Crooks, as their two versions of events were quite well synced. Only then Mr. Munroe paused for the first time before giving his answer, and he got a real thoughtful look on his face, and finally he continued.

"Yeah, Crooksy, he said he think he knocked her the fuck out."

I saw the judge raise her gavel into the air, only she didn't slam it down, because as it turns out you are able to swear as much as you want if you are reciting evidence of things that were actually said. Only then Mr. Crooks stood up from where he was seated and started calling Mr. Munroe a, "fucking rat," and that allowed the gavel to come down for real this time.

"Order!" called the judge, as one of the prisoner escorts pulled Mr. Crooks back down into his seat.

I could see that this was quite a surprise to Mr. Crooks and his lawyer, based on the now hurried conversation that was taking place between them, and perhaps to the prosecutor as well, as she had a happy look on her face.

Once order had been restored, the examination continued.

"Mr. Munroe, you were saying that Mr. Crooks had said that he think he knocked her out. Did he elaborate?"

"Well, what he said before, about her bein' beat up already. He said that, too. Said she was beat up good, crying on the floor or something. Then he walked in on her and she started screamin, so he knocked her out."

"Did he say anything more?"

"He said he hoped he didn't kill her."

Again Mr. Crooks jumped to his feet and called Mr. Munroe a, "fucking rat," which seemed to be something that Mr. Crooks liked to say. Then the gavel. And I think that it was safe to say by then that I wasn't the judge's least favorite person in the room anymore.

Once order was restored, Mr. Munroe's lawyer sat down, and Mr. Crooks' lawyer shot to his feet to begin his cross-examination. Mr. Crooks' lawyer called Mr. Munroe a liar, saying that he was just trying to save his own skin, and suggesting that he was willing to frame an innocent man in order to do it. For his part, Mr. Munroe didn't get too bent out of shape about the allegations. He just said how he liked, "Crooksy," and even if he hit her, he believed that she was beat up before, and how maybe it wasn't that blow that did her in.

By the time it got to the prosecutor, she only questioned Mr. Munroe about his own knowledge, and why he didn't come forward to the police, given Mr. Crooks's confession. To this, Mr. Munroe simply stated, "I liked Crooksy," and that he wasn't even sure that Mr. Crooks had killed her, based on what he'd said.

"But surely you must have known," said the prosecutor, "once you read it in the newspaper?"

"I don't read no papers, ma'am."

"Then when you saw it in the news?"

"Don't watch the news, neither."

I could see that she was becoming frustrated.

"Then when you were arrested for murder, along with Mr. Crooks. Did it happen to cross your mind then?"

"Yes, ma'am, it did."

"And then why didn't you say anything about it until now, pray tell?"

Mr. Munroe leaned back in the witness box. "Like I said, I like Crooksy. I didn't know it'd get this far. But here we are, and my ass is on the line, too. Crooksy'll understand."

Only it looked as if "Crooksy" didn't understand so much, as much it looked like he wanted to make Mr. Munroe as red and open as Mrs. Baker. That was when he jumped to his feet again and called Mr. Munroe a rat and a liar, and again he had to be restrained.

"Is there anything else you left out?" asked the prosecutor.

"Yeah, I'm real sorry about Herbert. Neither me or Crooksy touched him. Least I didn't, an I figure Crooksy woulda told me. I didn't hurt the lady. And I definitely didn't hurt Herbert."

This time there were no insults or objections or demonstrations of any sort, just a strange silence as if nobody could really believe what they'd just heard, and finally Mr. Munroe stood up and walked out of the witness box, his shackles clanking as he did, and with that, we were told that the evidence was completed.

Chapter 20

Closing submissions would commence the following day, and then we would be sequestered. This gave me one more night home with Donna and Toby and Molly before I would be locked away in a hotel with these other eleven people.

Shelley's sister had left immediately following our release, so I hadn't had the opportunity to follow up on our earlier conversation. I had somehow ended up in a conversation with the Adventurer and the nurse, and he was telling us about a time that he fought a kangaroo, and I couldn't help but wonder what issue could possibly come between a man and a kangaroo that would necessitate it. Then I started wondering if it was a male or a female kangaroo, and if it was a female kangaroo, if there was a joey in the pouch, and how maybe even the joey had become involved in the fight in some limited fashion, and it was only after I'd come out of my wondering that I could see that Shelley's sister had left.

I made it to my car and drove home without incident, and after walking through the front door, Toby came running in from the kitchen yelling, "Daddy, Daddy," as he was wont to do. Molly came running too, only she wasn't saying Daddy as much as she was barking, and though she could conceivably have been expressing some thoughtful communication that I simply couldn't understand, the chances are that it was just excited yet meaningless gibberish.

Donna soon approached wearing an apron and wiping her hands with a towel, which presumably meant that she was making dinner, and the normalcy of it all made me feel warm inside, especially given the contrast of listening to murder-talk and slammed gavels.

"Peters called," she said.

"Did he say what he wanted?" I asked, as I tried unsuccessfully to fend off Toby and Molly's advances.

"He just wanted to check in to see how the trial was going and when you might be expected back."

Pressuring their employees to come back to work was a trait common to most bosses, even the better bosses such as Mr. Peters. Gordon called this "Management Disease," as if it was a condition that could be diagnosed and treated by a doctor. According to Gordon, almost all bosses become infected by it after enough time in their positions. He said that the performance pressures caused bosses to behave in rude or unsympathetic ways, for example, urging their better employees to come back too soon when they were sick or bereaved.

In this case, while we had some good salespeople like Gordon and Gary and a few others, it hurt sales when I wasn't able to work. Not only that, but they had to pay me my average salary while I was away.

"The evidence concluded today," I said, after finally removing my shoes and entering further inside the house. "Tomorrow there will be closing submissions and then we will be sequestered."

"Do you know for how long?"

"It is difficult to say. I expect it could be days."

"Peters won't like that," she said, and I agreed.

The more I thought about it, the more I thought that Gordon was probably correct because even a good person such as Mr. Peters didn't seem to care so much that a woman had been brutally slain in her own master bedroom, as much as he was concerned that he might not sell enough vacuums to keep his own bosses happy, who would likely have been long-infected by the management disease themselves.

"Well, Peters can just fuck off," said Donna. She mouthed the last words quietly so Toby couldn't hear, and while I felt that she likely wouldn't have spoken so brazenly if Mr. Peters had been present, as I had gotten to know Donna better over the years, I couldn't be sure of that.

Toby kept saying, "Daddy come see," as he took my hand and pulled me toward the den, where he had been playing with his Legos. Toby had several policemen and a dog setup outside of a building, and he said the building was a bank, and that a bad man was inside, even though he wasn't so much inside as he was standing on the roof, which is where Toby had placed him.

"This is Max," he said, pointing to the police dog, and I couldn't help but notice his enthusiasm as he said it.

"And who is this?" I said, pointing to one of the policemen.

"That's just the policeman," he said.

"Does he have a name?"

Toby seemed to hem and haw at this, and finally said that his name was Fred, but unlike naming the dog, it was not a full-throated commitment. Then I asked about the other two policemen, and though the effort seemed to trouble him, he finally named them Sam and Linda, and I realized how I hadn't even considered that one of the policemen might actually be a policewoman. I had read about "casual misogyny" in the newspaper, which is a term that described how we unintentionally perpetuate gender stereotypes by our words and conduct, and my presuming that all of the police were indeed men seemed to be an example of that. And then I thought about how perhaps this was in turn going to turn Toby into a casual misogynist himself, only when I looked over at him, he was making simple, "bang bang," noises and clumsily hitting one of the figures on the ground, and I figured that in that moment he was likely not thinking about very much of anything at all, so I decided not to be too fussed about it.

I was preparing to leave the matter entirely, when my head got stuck on the name "Sam", and it occurred to me that there might not only be one, but two policewomen, if Sam was short for Samantha, and while I recognized that it didn't matter one way or the other because it was just a piece of plastic, and the genders had just been casually ascribed, I asked Toby if Sam were a boy or a girl, and he said "a boy" and I couldn't help but feel some sense of relief as a result of this clarity.

Donna had made lasagna and garlic bread for dinner, and after our meal we walked around the neighborhood with Molly, and that night Donna helped me to achieve it, but not before I'd told Toby and Molly and Donna that I loved them.

I said it because it was true.

Chapter 21

I arrived at court early on Monday, finding only the student and the old woman having arrived ahead of me. I sat down next to the old woman. And while I ordinarily preferred to isolate myself in social situations, she had been kind to me on that first day when she came to my defense against juror number four, and I had noticed that she mostly kept to herself throughout these proceedings and wondered if perhaps she was lonely.

I think that old people intimidate most people, even though most old people are harmless and actually carry a wealth of wisdom and experience. My parents used to tell me that old people were like unopened gifts and how you just had to sit down and talk to unwrap them, so I decided to listen to my parents that morning and unwrap the old woman.

"Good morning," I said, sitting down beside her.

"Well, good morning to you, as well."

Her voice was old and hoarse, but not in a bad way.

"It would seem that we have heard all the evidence in the case."

"Yes," she said, before adding, "It certainly is a lot to think about."

"Is this the first time that you have served on a jury?"

"It is," she said. "You know, there was a time we couldn't sit on juries."

I felt that it was strange to hear that old people couldn't sit on juries since they had a lot of knowledge and life experience and most of them were retired, so they could sit around all day listening to the lawyers ask "what happened next" and argue amongst themselves without being too fussed about it. Only then she clarified that it was women who couldn't sit on juries when she was young, and I realized it had nothing to do with old people at all, except maybe for old women.

"Never got the chance until now," she said.

I saw how she'd brought her wrinkled hands together, and it looked like she might be in some level of pain or discomfort from arthritis by the way that she was holding them.

"Once we hear their closing submissions, we will be sequestered," I said.

"Yes, they said that. I just hope we aren't away too long because I'll miss my Daisy."

I concluded correctly that this was a pet, rather than a single flower, and even if it wasn't much of an achievement, I still felt some small sense of pride in having extrapolated correctly from the limited information I had been provided.

She told me that Daisy was her French poodle and how they didn't like to be away from one another for very long, but how she had already been informed that the hotel where we were to be sequestered did not allow pets of any kind, except for service or police dogs, and since Daisy the French poodle wasn't necessary to guide juror number eight around, or was likely to smell out bombs from mysterious packages, it seemed that her attendance would be unwelcome.

"Since my husband passed, Daisy has always been there for me."

She then removed a photograph from her purse to show me Daisy. She looked like a good little dog, so I told her so, and that made the old woman smile.

"I can't bear to be apart from her for too long."

"I suppose we may be deliberating for some time," I said.

"Not if you ask some of these people," she said, and she said "these people" rather disdainfully, suggesting that they had already made their mind up about the two men's guilt.

"We are duty bound to consider all of the evidence, including the submissions of counsel," I said. I said this because it is what we were told at the start by the judge, and I had no reason to believe that she intended to mislead us.

"Well, that is very responsible of you. Such a nice young man." She reached out and set her hand on mine as she said it, and there was something very respectful and comforting about it as she did, that it didn't bother me as it usually might have.

It was about that time that Shelley's sister entered the room. Our eyes met for just a moment before she found a spot by the wall on her own.

Things had not been the same between us since the night that she may or may not have helped me to achieve it two times in room number three, and while I recognized that it all might have just been in my head, I felt that it was necessary to be certain.

I said goodbye to the old woman and approached Shelley's sister. Her red hair seemed wet, like she had just come from the shower, and she had dark circles under her eyes.

"Hello," I said.

"Hey."

"I did not get to see you before you left yesterday."

"Nah, I slipped out as soon as I could. I had a long night of work and wanted to get a nap in."

"I see."

"I must look like shit."

I wanted to say that she was mistaken, but the fact was that she looked rather haggard. I was always told by my parents that it wasn't right to lie to people, and even if it might hurt their feelings, most people would actually appreciate an honest answer so that they might have an opportunity to fix what was wrong. So instead of disagreeing with her, I just told her that she looked "tired."

She just laughed and said that was "very polite" of me.

"Why did you work so late?"

"'Cause I figure we may be here for a while, and I can't afford to miss too many shifts."

"The judge said that our employers must pay us a wage equal to our average salary since we are here by law."

She just looked up at me, as if incredulously.

"If you saw the place I worked…"

She said a few other things about her employer after that, but I didn't pay any attention, because she had just revealed in her answer that I had never actually been to The Rocksteady, thus confirming that the entire set of events Friday night had been in my mind. This pleased me since it meant that I had not been unfaithful to Donna in real life, but only in my mind, and while I figured that being figuratively unfaithful might still be sub-optimal, I concluded that it was still better than the alternative.

"Hey!" she said.

"Yes?"

"Where'd you go?"

She was asking me where my thoughts had drifted off to, so I apologized and said that I was just thinking about "things," which was as specific as I felt that I could be under the circumstances.

"Anyway, it's not so bad there. They keep us safe, at least. They don't let anyone get rough with us. Kick out the creeps. That sort of thing."

While her employer did not sound particularly reputable in some ways, it at least pleased me that they kept the women safe. The fact was that if certain women chose to make their living as a result of using their bodies, they deserved the right to be safe and secure in their environment. The way it was in life, women already faced enough danger from their boyfriends and fiancées and husbands, so it didn't seem like too much to ask that they at least have safety at work.

Within the next fifteen minutes, the remainder of the jurors had arrived, and soon afterwards we were led into the courtroom and seated in our usual positions. The judge then invited the counsel to make their closing submissions.

Mr. Crooks's lawyer went first. He stood up in an animated fashion just as he always did, walking briskly to the podium. He then highlighted, with a raised voice, how the prosecution's case was flimsy and circumstantial, and that the actual culprit in this crime was most certainly the husband, Mr. Baker, and how his client was just a patsy.

He then went on to say that Mr. Munroe's testimony should be rejected as it was convenient and self-serving. He said that, clearly, Mr. Munroe was scared that they would be convicted for a crime that they did not do, and so he must have seen putting the finger on his partner as a way out.

"He is scared, and he is singing for his supper," cried Mr. Crooks's counsel, which seemed to be a rather clever way to describe it. He also pointed aggressively at Mr. Munroe as he said it.

Finally, he stated that there was good reason for his client's DNA to be there, as he had readily admitted to having been all through the home during the course of the burglary. He said that his client should be found guilty in relation to the break and enter, but certainly no murder.

Mr. Munroe's counsel went next. He highlighted how both Mr. Crooks and Mr. Munroe had asserted that his client was the getaway driver, that he was only briefly in the home, and how he never went upstairs.

"You cannot be a party to something that you do not know is happening," said the lawyer calmly, and while he conceded that Mr. Crooks admitted to his client he hit Mrs. Baker, he could not be sure of the gravity of the injury, and they had already left the scene when the disclosure was made.

At most, said his lawyer, he is guilty of being a party to a burglary, and of bad judgment in keeping silent about Mr. Crooks's admission.

Finally, it was the prosecutor's turn. She stood up calmly and walked to the podium, then re-capped all of the evidence piece by piece. She urged us to believe that the husband had discovered his wife just as he said he had and urged us to reject the extraordinary coincidence that he would murder his wife in cold blood, only to have two men fortuitously break into the home that very night so that he could pin the murder on them.

"Are these men the two most unlucky men in the country?" she asked. "Maybe on the planet?"

She said not to be distracted by the husband's prior allegation of violence, which had not resulted in a conviction, for it was only that…an allegation.

"Do not be fooled," she said. "Focus on the evidence in this case, and use your own common sense."

"And the dog," she said. "Do not forget how they treated the dog. Beating it and locking it in a room. Brutal, sadistic behavior. Yet we are to believe, as their lawyers urge, that they are not capable of violence?"

Finally, with respect to Mr. Munroe, she urged us not to believe his lie. That he had tried his best to distance himself from knowledge of the murder, but to no avail.

"Believe the admission by Mr. Crooks that he had 'knocked her the fuck out'. But do not believe that it occurred only after they had driven away. Do not believe that Mr. Munroe was ever in doubt about her condition. Believe what really happened, which is that he knew she had been killed, and he acted as their getaway driver knowing as much."

And with that, she invited us to return verdicts of guilt on all charges, then strode confidently back to her seat.

Chapter 22

For the remainder of the day, the judge read us a series of instructions. These were similar to what we had heard at the outset, about our duties and responsibilities as jurors, though there were additional details and a general re-cap of the evidence.

It was late afternoon when that was completed, and then three jury attendants pledged an oath to watch over us during our deliberations. We then convened back in the jury room to make our final preparations for sequester. Some people had already brought overnight bags and suitcases and left them in the jury room. Others had left their bags or cases in their cars, as I had. Only, we were no longer allowed to go anywhere on our own, so those of us who needed to retrieve our bags from our cars were chaperoned there one by one by the attendants. We were told that this was how it was going to be for the duration of the sequester, except when we were in our hotel rooms.

Since I had to get my own bag from the trunk of the car, the one female jury attendant accompanied me outside, after she had done the same for the nurse. She told me that her name was Nancy. We had only just stepped outside when I asked her how long we might be sequestered.

"Oh, it depends. There is no set rule for these things."

"I see."

"I have seen it take a few hours," she added, "and I have also seen it take ten days."

"My boss would like to see me return to work."

She didn't say anything to that.

"I sell vacuums. We have other people who can also sell vacuums, but most don't sell as many as I do."

"You must be a very fine salesperson," she said, and I said that this was probably true.

We had just arrived at my car where it was parked in the parking lot of the courthouse. I opened the trunk and took out an overnight bag that I had prepared the night before with Donna and Toby, and I believe even Molly had tried to help in her limited capacity, by lying next to it.

"Will my car be safe here overnight?" I asked, after locking it.

"There's cameras and even a security guard," she responded, "So it should be safe here. Safe as anywhere else, at least."

It wasn't much of a car, but it was important to get me to and from work, and to drop Toby off at school, and to pick up things like groceries. I was thinking of these things, and then I decided to say them.

"Yes, I could see that as being important," she said.

Nancy mostly just nodded and agreed with everything I said, which seemed quite polite and professional. I was thinking about asking her if this was part of her training, only then I thought that might undermine her if she was just a naturally polite and professional person, so I decided not to. That was also when we were just returning to the front steps of the courthouse, and I saw juror number four being escorted by one of the other jury attendants. He had a green sack slung over his shoulder, like he was in the army.

I avoided eye contact with him, which was something that my parents and counselors had taught me was a good idea with those that triggered uncomfortably strong emotions, and the fact was that I had strongly mixed emotions with respect to the retired policeman. While at first I felt he was a cruel, vile man, I later repented killing him in my dreams, and even felt sufficient guilt to apologize to him in real life. Only now that more time had passed, I felt a strange emotion welling up inside me.

The relief I had originally felt after learning that I had not killed him, had now been strangely and slowly supplanted by a growing feeling of dissatisfaction, and a desire or emptiness that I hadn't felt before. It was only in that moment that I truly appreciated how strongly I felt this feeling, and how I even felt that I had been deprived of something, and how strongly I felt the urge to complete the task that I had previously only imagined.

But it wasn't just that.

Shelley's sister had just walked past me and smiled warmly in my direction, and this too felt like a conquest that had been snatched away from me, and as my gaze fixated on her shiny red hair and her dancer's figure, I couldn't help thinking about the desires that had all welled up in my mind in that moment, to achieve it with Shelley's sister, and to make juror number four red and open.

It is possible that all of these feelings would have drifted away peacefully on their own, had I not now been forced to travel with them to a hotel, where we would be shut together in sequester.

But as strange as all of that was, it was perhaps not the strangest thing of all. For as I reflected back on all of this, once the trial was over, and once I had done what I had done, I couldn't help but think back on the exceptional unlikelihood of two simple truths, interwoven in one existence…

Whoever knew that a child's toy could exonerate, and a kind connection lead to murder?

PART TWO
THE SEQUESTER

Company Closing Techniques
1. The Columbo Close
2. The Benjamin Franklin Close
3. The Alternative Close
4. The Compromise Close
5. The Imaginary Close
6. The By Mistake Close
7. The Follow The Leader Close
8. The Apology Close
9. The Sharp Angle Close
10. The Hard Close
11. The Assumptive Close
12. The Now Or Never Close

Chapter 1

As we boarded the bus, they collected all of our phones and other devices that were capable of accessing the Internet or otherwise connecting with the outside world. We were told by the judge that they would be doing so, and that for a proper sequester they had to ensure that we were sufficiently cut off from others so as not to hear any news or commentary about the case such that it might impact on our deliberations. I remember when they got to the old lady, there was nothing to take from her, which in some ways made me think that she was living in the past, but in other ways made me think that she might be the only person living in the present.

I sat next to the garbage collector once we got inside. He looked to be in his late twenties, and he had tattoos on his tanned arms.

"It will be interesting to begin deliberations," I said, feeling that this was a decent enough icebreaker and that it would be sufficient to satisfy proper social etiquette. I would have been satisfied if he'd just nodded, or even chosen not to respond at all, but as it turned out he apparently had something to say.

"Yeah, not sure how long it will be, though."

"You believe it will go quickly?" I asked.

"Don't you?"

It was clear that the garbage collector had already made up his mind about the guilt or innocence of the two men. I, on the other hand, had been doing my best to listen to all of the evidence and follow the instructions of the judge. She had admonished us from jumping to any conclusions until we had had the opportunity to review the entirety of the evidence and to discuss the matter amongst ourselves, and in this way I felt that the garbage collector was acting prematurely.

"I believe we will have to review and debate the evidence," I said.

"You mean, review how two men broke into a house and how they found the homeowner dead, and how they got caught selling her stuff?" Then he laughed a bit under his breath.

I could see that the matter was going to require some level of negotiation as it was clear that some of the jurors were already convinced of the guilt of the two men, and while I did not have experience in mediation or dispute resolution, my company had taught us various psychological tricks to influence people to buy our vacuums. These were psychological ploys that our company had taught us had been scientifically proven to work in overcoming objections and enhancing sales, and I thought if they worked well enough to convince people to purchase vacuums that they might not necessarily want or need, then they might work equally well to ensure that my fellow jurors responsibly considered their verdict.

One of the closing tactics we learned was called The Alternative Close. For example, you would narrow down the customer's interest to two vacuums, and then ask them which one they wanted between the two, without asking them if they actually wanted to buy one of them. By not leaving the option of not purchasing, customers overwhelmingly selected to buy one of the two vacuums.

This was a psychological trick that our company said was scientifically proven to work, so I decided to attempt to deploy it.

"I suppose they are either innocent or they are guilty," I said, at which point he quickly responded that he thought they were probably guilty.

As it turns out, The Alternative Close worked much better for choosing between two vacuums than it did in choosing between guilt and innocence, which were two fundamentally opposite concepts, rather than purchase alternatives that were both equally good for the salesperson, so I felt it best to avoid that tactic going forward, or to at least be more responsible with its deployment.

"I understand that you are a garbage collector?" I said, in an effort to change the conversation, which had grown uncomfortable.

"That's right."

He didn't say anything further, and while I felt this was an opportunity to let the conversation harmlessly peter out, I also felt that it deserved some follow up comment, given that I had just raised it.

"I have often found it to be an inaccurate job description as it suggests that you hoard the garbage, rather than simply relocate it for disposal."

"Hoard the garbage?" he asked.

"I believe that if you were called a garbage relocator, it would more accurately reflect the work that you do."

He laughed when I said it.

"Should you take any of it home with you after your shift," I said, "I would consider the matter differently."

He looked at me queerly after I said it. "You serious?"

"I believe it is inaccurate," I said.

This time he didn't laugh. He just shook his head as he turned his head away, so I took this as an opportunity to end the conversation.

I have often found it difficult to speak with people, and this was just another one of those times. I could even tell by how he was seated and the look on his face that he felt uncomfortable, and even I started to feel that way too, but then it wasn't long after that when we arrived to the hotel, so we didn't have to drive in an uncomfortable silence for very long.

Chapter 2

It wasn't much of a hotel.

The carpet was dated, the hallway lighting was dim, and there was a light bulb flickering by the ice machine That said, my room number was seventeen, which was a number I liked well enough, so I felt that my thoughts wouldn't be bothered by a bad room number and how it probably wouldn't occupy my thoughts much more than it currently was in thinking about how it probably wouldn't.

The room had a queen-size bed and a chair and a television, only the television had been unplugged or otherwise deactivated. They had told us they had to do this to ensure that we didn't see or hear anything on the local news that might influence our verdicts. Even the telephones had been taken out of the rooms.

We were also told that one of Nancy and the two other jury attendants would always be awake and positioned in the hallway, while the other two would sleep or rest as needed. While they apparently felt this was necessary to ensure that none of us snuck out or engaged in any prohibited conduct, I felt that the threat of me sneaking out to be with other people was marginal; in fact, Donna usually had to manipulate or coerce me in some fashion in order to secure such behavior. However, the jury attendants couldn't possibly know this, and there were eleven other people who might not be quite so averse to interacting with other members of society, so I felt their precautions to be sound.

My room was an adjoining room, and hardly twenty minutes had passed before I heard a knock at the adjoining door, which I unlocked and opened to discover the student.

"Hey, neighbor."

She was already in her pajamas as she stood in the doorway.

"I never thanked you for what you did, you know, for standing up for me."

She was talking about when she had been verbally accosted by juror number four.

"It was not right of him to speak to you that way."

"Yeah, well, most people just watched."

"Many people are uncomfortable with confrontation," I said.

"They're cowards, you mean."

I wasn't sure of this, so I didn't respond.

"Well, I guess we have to find a way to work together now."

"May I ask you a question?" I said, after agreeing with her last comment, and she consented without much contemplation.

"I noticed that you were reading a book before, in the room. Have you completed the book?"

"Nah, I got sidetracked, but I brought it with me."

"Do you know what page you are on?"

She looked at me quizzically when I asked it, then shrugged and walked over to her nightstand, where I saw the same book as before. As she brought it back, I saw that the bookmark was not too far off from where it had been before, and when she opened it up, she said that she was on page 212. This satisfied me that I was indeed correct that she had at least been on page 172 when I had first seen it, and this gave me a sense of pride in my abilities.

"Have you enjoyed it?" I asked.

"Yeah, it's pretty good. It's a book about how people take themselves way too seriously in life, and how life is rather absurd and ridiculous and pointless, so you might as well just take a deep breath and enjoy it."

This seemed like something of an oversimplification, but then I also saw merit to the position.

"Anyway, I just wanted to say hi and to say thanks," she said.

This was her way of concluding the conversation. Most people would preface a sentence with the word "Anyway" when they were looking to end a certain discussion, change topics, or simply extricate themselves from a situation, and not only did I feel that she had used it appropriately in that moment, I was also relieved that she was prepared to conclude the conversation as I had little else to say in that moment.

I told her that she was welcome and to have a good night, and then she closed the door behind her and I heard her turn the lock from her side, and I thought about how not only was she thankful, but how she was also careful, because for all she knew I was a killer who might do her harm, which I was, but I wouldn't. However, I still felt the precaution reflected well on her, and how her parents would probably be proud of how they had raised her. Only then I figured that even if she didn't lock the door, and she was slaughtered in her sleep, they could still probably be proud of how they'd raised her, so it made me rescind my earlier conclusion that the locking of the door might have impacted on their level of pride.

I then went to bed and tried to sleep but was unsuccessful, which is to say that I believe I was successful at the trying part, but not the actual sleeping part.

It was nearly eleven when I got dressed and went into the hallway. The male jury attendant was seated outside on a chair. He rose to his feet once I closed the door behind me.

"Anything wrong, sir?"

I said that there wasn't, and that I just wanted to take a walk.

"Afraid I need to get someone to go with you," he said.

"I see."

"We have to make sure you aren't interfered with. That sort of thing."

I couldn't imagine who would want to interfere with me, only then I thought how associates of either accused party might be lurking about and might wish to influence our vote. It got me to thinking about what, if anything, could be said or done to me that might make me vote against my principles, but nothing immediately came to mind. Only then I thought that perhaps if someone threatened my family or Molly that it could potentially sway my decision. I hadn't included the cat in this equation, because I somehow didn't envision criminal associates threatening the cat, nor did I think it would alter my vote even if they did.

The jury attendant walked over to one of the rooms and knocked on the door, and it wasn't long before the woman not named Nancy came out. She was a large woman with curly hair.

"How may I be of service, sir?"

"I would like to take a walk," I said.

"Yes, of course, be happy to. I'll just grab a sweater."

She went back inside her room and came out wearing a knit sweater, and then we both walked down the hallway toward the elevators. Once we got to the first floor, I noticed that there was a hotel bar off to the side, and I asked if perhaps we could stop in for a drink.

"I'm afraid not."

"Sometimes I take a drink if I am having difficulty sleeping," I said.

"Perhaps once we get back we could have a glass of wine or beer sent up to your room then?"

This seemed like a sensible solution, so I agreed to it rather quickly without further negotiation.

"My name is Helen," she said as we moved outside the front doors and out onto the sidewalk. We then set out walking in no particular direction.

This particular hotel was in a darker, quieter part of the city, which I presume was done intentionally so as to limit interference with the jurors.

I asked Helen the same question that I had asked Nancy, about how long it might take, and she gave me much the same ambiguous answer.

"So it could take days?" I asked.

"It could. It will take as long as it needs."

"I believe some of the jurors have already made up their minds."

She didn't respond to this, except to say that she was not allowed to discuss the case with me for fear it could influence my decision, which seemed a responsible approach.

We walked around the block, and the night air was cool and pleasant. After about ten minutes, we went back inside and got into the elevator. That was when I started thinking about Shelley's sister.

"Are we allowed to visit one another, in the hotel?"

"Other jurors?" she asked, to which I nodded.

"Well, there's no rule against it."

She then asked me if there was someone I wanted to speak to specifically, which I denied, even though this was a lie, as I wished to see Shelley's sister, though I couldn't say what I would do once I was there. The fact was that I was feeling incredibly conflicted about my desires regarding both her and juror number four, and what I wanted to do with each of them, which involved varying aspects of physicality as applied to varying aspects of their anatomies. And while I may have committed murder on occasion in the past, I had only ever cheated on Donna in my mind; I had yet to cheat on her with my body, which was probably what really mattered.

"Anyway," she said, as we stepped out of the elevator and back to my door, "I hope you enjoyed the walk," which I said that I had, after having now been "anywayed" twice in the past twenty minutes. I told her that I also had enjoyed the walk, and then I thanked her for her service, and I do believe she appreciated it just as much as the other jury attendant when I had slipped him the note with my question.

She also had a beer sent up just as promised, after which I went back to bed and tried to sleep, realizing only the next morning when my eyes opened and it was light out that I'd been successful in more than the trying.

Chapter 3

I believe that it might help if we were to go around the table to hear from each person," I said, after the nurse asked how we might get started.

Following breakfast, we were shuttled back to the courthouse, where we convened in the jury room just after ten a.m. The accountant had volunteered to be the jury foreperson, since nobody else wanted to do it, so he seated himself at the head of the table, which was also very convenient, since he was juror #1. We then seated ourselves around the table in clockwise fashion, in the same order as our juror numbers, so it ended up looking like this in my mind, though I suppose it may have looked a bit different to my actual eyes:

I had suggested that we might go once around the table because I had seen something similar in a movie starring Henry Fonda, and since it seemed to work in that case, I thought that it might work here. I even explained the basis for my suggestion, thinking that it might help people better understand, only juror number four laughed when I said it.

"Yeah, yeah, Herman Melville and Henry Fonda, how 'bout we stay in the real world for a while, eh fella?"

I thought that it was not only inaccurate of him to say it—because while those things may only have been books or plays, they both clearly existed in the real world—but I also thought it was rude of him to say it in the manner that he did.

"Look, now, there's no reason to get excited." This was the Adventurer seated three seats to my left, who often attempted to play peacemaker when juror number four would say something rude or insensitive.

Before I could respond, the accountant said, "I think it's a good idea. How about a once around the table, just to see what people are thinking, and then we can go from there?"

I saw most everyone's heads nodding up and down and then I realized mine was doing the same, so then we agreed to take a preliminary vote to see where people stood.

It didn't take long to do it, and in the end these were the results that I scratched down into my notepad:

Peter Crooks:	Guilty	Not-Guilty
Burglary	12	0
Murder	11	1

Sheldon Munroe:	Guilty	Not-Guilty
Burglary	12	0
Murder	6	6
Accessory after the fact to murder	10	2
Cruelty to animals	11	1

It was unanimous that they were each guilty of burglary, as they had clearly broken and entered with the intent to steal from the home and had admitted as much in their testimony. In fact, both lawyers had invited us to find them each guilty of that offence.

The next and most serious charge was the murder of Mrs. Baker. Everyone believed that Mr. Crooks was probably guilty of this offence, myself included. It was only Shelley's sister who had a doubt. When asked why she was not convinced, she just stated, "I know men," before adding, "especially married men," but then she said no more than that.

The murder vote on Mr. Munroe was split right down the middle. I was among those who had a reasonable doubt about his involvement, as were Shelley's sister, the student, the old woman, the accountant, and the dentist.

The last two charges were for Mr. Munroe alone. Even if we had a doubt that he took part in the murder, if we were satisfied that he was sufficiently aware that Mr. Crooks had committed the murder, but then helped him get away from the scene, then we were told he could be found guilty of being an accessory after the fact. Only myself and Shelley's sister voted not-guilty on this charge.

The final charge was for beating the dog Herbert. Only the student believed that he was not guilty of this offence.

"Well, now we know where we stand," said the accountant, who had also made his own notes on his own pad of paper.

"So where do we go from here?"

It was the dentist who said it, a black woman in her forties with short black hair with red streaks. She had been largely quiet up to this point in the proceedings, sometimes talking with other jurors about her two young sons or her dog Bandit, but otherwise she would sit quietly in the jury room looking through the notes that she had made throughout the case. I never did hear the names of her two sons, but she did talk an awful lot about Bandit, and how she missed being away from him, and how he was a good little boy, and based on how fondly she spoke of him, I had no problem concluding beyond a reasonable doubt that he surely was.

"Well," said the old woman in her weathered voice, "since the young lady believes that neither man is guilty of murder, maybe we should start there?"

I watched as Shelley's sister brought her hands together and set them into a wringing motion, as if maybe the thought of speaking openly about it made her nervous. Only then several others joined in and asked if she would care to comment on why she felt neither man was guilty, since she was the only holdout on Mr. Crooks.

And so this was how we began our deliberations.

Chapter 4

L ike I said before," she started, her voice low. "I know men. Not just from talking to the other girls, but what I hear from the men themselves. The things they say about their partners."

"What sort of things?" asked the accountant.

"Just little comments. Belittling stuff. A lot of anger."

"So some men hurt your feelings, and you want to let this Crooks guy off the hook?"

That was juror number four, whose tone was rude and dismissive. I had already felt myself holding the pen tighter after he'd told me to stay in the real world, and then I felt my grip tighten even further by how he had just spoken to Shelley's sister.

"I'm just saying that it could have been the husband, that's all."

"But is that enough to exonerate these two men?" asked the CEO.

"Not to mention," said the baker, "that the allegations we heard about the husband, it sounds like they didn't go anywhere. The lady—the deceased, I mean—she herself said that she lied."

"My sister Shelley, she's a cop. She tells me all the time how often abuse happens, and how often women will change their stories once the trial comes, or try to get the charges dropped. Maybe she's scared of him. Maybe she doesn't have anywhere else to go. There are lots of reasons."

"It's true," said the nurse with the stern voice. "I see it all the time. Abused women do cover for their abusive partners. They lie to protect them."

I knew this to be true as well, not only because I had read this same thing in a magazine article, but because I had also seen my neighbor go through domestic abuse at the hand of her boyfriend, and I had heard her making excuses for him and how he wasn't such a bad person, and I believe the abuse might have escalated further had I not stabbed him fourteen times in the stomach when I'd killed him in mostly self-defense.

"Is there anything that we can do to help satisfy you that it was not the husband?" asked the dentist with the red streaks, who had suddenly become much more talkative since our deliberations had begun, as if perhaps she'd been saving her voice up for when it mattered, and who was trying to identify her specific objection to finding Mr. Crooks guilty.

My company had taught us that when facing an objection, you could find out how entrenched the customer was by offering up a false piece of information, to see if the customer would correct you. This was called The By-Mistake Close. For example, if they said that they were looking to buy a new vacuum by the end of the week, you might comment on how you understand that it was important that they secure one by the end of the month. If the customer corrected you and said, "No, I need it by the end of the week," then it suggested that they had emotionally committed to the purchase, and it perhaps even pushed them into settling upon the purchase in their own mind, whereas if they did not correct you, it might demonstrate that they really didn't care what you had to say.

I had always felt this to be a risky strategy because you also ran the risk of looking incompetent, or lacking in basic short-term memory skills, such as the square card game that Donna and I would play with Toby, whereby we would flip over two tiles at a time of ladybugs and bicycles and armadillos to see if he could find matches.

I once tried The By-Mistake Close with a customer who had said that they wished to have a vacuum cleaner that was red, and when I was unsure if she really wanted to purchase it, I confirmed that she wished to have a vacuum that was yellow, at which point she said that it was clear I was not even listening to her and hung up. I remember thinking that I might have had more success if I had used "maroon" or "burgundy" as my mistake color, and how selecting a color that was so diametrically opposed to red might not have been the best strategy, but then I figured what was done was done and there was no point beating myself up over it. And while that had been the last time I had attempted to use The By-Mistake Close to ascertain the customer's level of interest in purchasing a vacuum, I thought that it might work here to gage how entrenched she was in her position.

"I believe that we cannot convince her otherwise, and that the men must be set free."

I said it rather suddenly and flatly, which is to say that I said it much the same as I said anything else.

Shelley's sister quickly corrected me that this was not the case, and that she just did not want us rushing into our decision, thus conceding that her objection was not final, and that she had perhaps even detached from her original objection in her own mind. In this way, I felt that I had successfully deployed The By-Mistake Close for the first time in my life, and feeling emboldened by this, I made a mental note to consider re-introducing it into my sales techniques once I returned to work.

I was just thinking of how I might do so when the baker said, "What if we looked at some of the exhibits?" as he looked up from beyond his tiny spectacles. "Go through them and see if that helps to resolve some of our doubts? I think we will have to, in any event, as we are rather divided on Mr. Munroe."

This seemed like a sensible suggestion, and it wasn't long before everyone had agreed, so we reached for the evidence bags one by one that had been lined up on a side table.

We started with the murder weapon.

Chapter 5

The murder weapon was a marble bookend shaped like a Rook. The Adventurer placed it in the center of the table so we all had a good view. It was still wrapped in a clear plastic evidence baggie, and there was dried blood flaked overtop the horse's head.

"Remember that they said it was normally kept downstairs," he said. "So, if you're the husband, why bring it from downstairs to kill her? Why not just kill her with a closer object, or perhaps wait until she comes downstairs? Mr. Crooks, however, likely had it in his hand as he was in the midst of stealing it."

Several people nodded when he said it. Then the baker reached out and picked it up.

"It's heavy," he said, moving it up and down in the air for added emphasis.

"I just think the husband would have covered it up better," added the old woman, shakily. "If the husband had done it, as you suspect, dear, wouldn't he have taken some time to cover things up, or maybe even to dispose of the body?"

"But you can say the same thing about the two burglars," responded Shelley's sister.

"I'm not so sure," said the CEO. "They knew that the person in the van could return home anytime. They had to rush. So it makes sense they would leave her on the floor and quickly leave with their bounty."

"And the husband could have just cancelled his meeting," added the old woman, only then Shelley's sister replied, "That might have made him look more suspicious."

Several of the other jurors took turns holding the bookend.

"It is pretty heavy," said the student, perhaps now swayed by Shelley's sister. "You think a burglar is going to throw this in a sack and lug it around the whole time they are robbing the place?"

"Why not?" said the CEO. "They take other heavy stuff, like computers. I'm sure it's worth something."

"And something else," said Shelley's sister, "why not just leave? I mean, they're petty criminals, right? They were careful to make sure nobody was home. Why not just leave when they came upon one of the homeowners?"

"You mean, why didn't they just say 'sorry for breaking into your house, we'll be on our way now'?" This was juror number four, and he laughed as he said it.

"What's so crazy about that? Better five years for burglary than life." That was when she finally turned and looked at me and asked, "What do you think?" as she pushed the bookend in my direction.

"I do not believe they would just leave," I said, after I'd cradled the object in my hand for a moment.

I saw a look on her face as if perhaps I had betrayed her. Only before either one of us could say anything else, juror number four said, "You get that from Dickens?" and then he started laughing.

I don't know if it was the fact that he was trying to make fun of me again, or the fact that he was doing it again openly in front of Shelley's sister, but something in me went wild with anger, and I stood up, the rook still clench-ed firmly in my hands, and even through the plastic evidence bag I could feel the grooves of the edges digging into my palms, only I didn't release it because I was so angry in that moment. I had been taught by my counselors that focusing on my sensations would allow me time to detach from obsessive thoughts, so I squeezed as hard as ever to try and feel something, only none of it mattered because I was already imagining juror number four as red and open, and I was thinking about how good it would feel to reach across the table and smash the heavy slab of marble into the side of his head, and how it would probably split open his skin and stun him, and how I would then crawl up over the table as he staggered in that spot and bring the object crashing down on the top of his skull with both hands and all the strength I could muster, and how it would either create a catastrophic fracture or break his neck or both.

"Whoa, easy there, fella."

I had already started into my breathing exercises by then, and between that and focusing on the sensations, I was able to disassociate from my violent thoughts, and that was when I saw that the Adventurer was beside me.

He'd come out of his chair, and he had even placed his palm on top of the object in the plastic evidence bag. It was only then, after a few more seconds, that I sufficiently regained my senses so as to move my hand down and deposit the rook gently back down on the table.

We then took a ten-minute break to help clear the air, but for at least half of those minutes I was still thinking of juror number four as red and open.

Chapter 6

I stepped outside the jury room in order to remove myself from the situation, which was something that my parents and counselors had encouraged me to do when I was younger and had urges of violence, and it usually worked to de-escalate the situation.

The bathroom was just down the hallway, and I was soon escorted there by one of the jury attendants, who waited outside, while inside I discovered a custodian cleaning the floors with a mop.

"Afternoon, sir," he said, which I felt was very polite of him even if it may not have been afternoon yet.

I stepped up to one of the urinals and did my business, even though I hadn't really needed to go, only then I figured that since I was able to go some, perhaps that meant that I did need to go all along, only I didn't need to go badly.

After I'd washed my hands, I apologized to the custodian for using the facilities he was currently trying to clean.

"That's what they're there for," he said.

"I suppose," I said. Then I bent over the sink and splashed some cool water on my face, which I had learned from one of my counselors was a refreshing sensation that would help trick my brain into detaching from the previous obsessive thought and thus help me to become calm.

Usually this worked, and by the time I'd patted my face down and straightened back up I felt better.

"Have you worked here long?" I asked the custodian, because I wasn't quite ready to return to the jury room.

"Oh, going on thirty years, I suppose. Thirty years, yessir."

I asked him if it was all at the courthouse, and he said that it was.

To me, this seemed like an awful long time to clean the same toilets and floors, and I couldn't help wonder if he found the work boring or monotonous, or both if those words meant the same thing. Instead, I just said, "That is a long time," to which he said, "Yessir, it sure is."

"May I ask you another question?" I said, still not prepared to leave the bathroom.

"Of course."

"Do you sometimes hear about jurors fighting? Or having disagreements?"

"Yessir, I see it all the time," said the custodian. He finally stopped mopping and looked at me directly.

"Have you ever heard of it becoming physical?"

"I have heard it happen a few times, yessir. Mostly it's just yelling and raised voices and such, but every once in a while, things get out of hand."

"I see."

"If you don't mind me asking," he said, pausing then and placing both hands around the top of the mop handle, "you having trouble within someone in there, sir?"

I told him that I was, and how one of the jurors was being rude and unprofessional with myself and some of the other jurors. I left out some of the other thoughts I was having, such as bludgeoning him to death with the very same murder weapon that had been used to kill Mrs. Baker because I felt that those details were likely extraneous to his ability to provide me advice.

"You wondering how to deal with it?" he asked.

"I suppose so," I said. "I had considered speaking to one of the jury attendants."

"Yeah, I suppose you could do that," he said, still leaning on his mop, only the way in which he said it suggested that he might pursue a different course of action, so I asked him what he would do if he were in my situation.

"Well, I'm just the custodian," he said, after a long pause, which seemed to be a rather self-deprecating way to summarize his chosen field of employment, "but if it was me, I think I might just wait until the end of the case, to keep things civilized, then settle up when nobody's looking."

"Keep things civilized?" I said.

"Yessir."

"Then settle up?"

"When nobody's looking." he said.

"I see."

"If it was me," he said before turning back to his mopping. "Of course, I'm just the custodian."

My father had told me, as I got a little older, that, "wisdom has no face." What he meant by that was that wise people come in all shapes and sizes, and how it could be a man or a woman, or an adult or a child, or rich or poor, or, as in this case, a gray-haired, mop-wielding custodian.

I was just preparing to leave when I said to him, "Thank you for your service," and this again immobilized him, and I watched as a smile spread onto his face, and he thanked me, with tears in his eyes, which he wiped back with his sleeve, and maybe even his doubts went washing away with them.

Chapter 7

By the time I was escorted back into the jury room I felt much better, and when we finally did resume our deliberations, the accountant had a few words about the pressure we were under with such an important decision, and that it was important that we all be patient and respect one another's opinions.

Shelley's sister had not looked at me or spoken to me since it happened, and I couldn't tell if it was the fact that she felt I had not supported her, or that perhaps that she had seen something in me that had scared her. But whatever the reason, she avoided looking at me for the rest of the morning.

"So where were we?" asked the accountant.

"The young lady had a doubt that it was the burglars who did it because she believes it may have been the husband. Is that fair, ma'am?"

That was the CEO, who sounded very professional, and had also provided an accurate recap of the current state of affairs.

"I'm telling you, the husband, he beat his wife."

"That may be the case," said the dentist with the red streaks, "but he's not the one on trial for domestic abuse."

"I'm just saying we have to think about it."

Others responded and said that we needed to be careful about giving undue weight to something that might have happened four years ago by turning it into an alibi for these two men. The debate went back and forth like this, all the way through lunch, which were sandwiches delivered into our room. By then I had been considering that we might draw up a chart. On the one side we could write what pieces of evidence supported each of the two men's guilt, discussing them as necessary. On the other side, what supported or raised a doubt about their innocence.

When I finally suggested it, the old woman said that this was, "an excellent idea, dear," and she patted me on my right arm as she said it, and it made me think of how I would pat Molly on her head and tell her that she was a good girl, which she certainly was, and how it felt good to receive such positive reinforcement and acknowledgment, and while in some contexts I might not appreciate being compared to a dog rather than a person, I think that in the vast majority of cases I would probably be OK with it, and I might even prefer it.

While I would have liked to take credit for the concept, especially after receiving the praise that I had, the fact was that this was just a sales technique my company taught us called The Benjamin Franklin Close. The Benjamin Franklin Close was a strategy whereby you drew a line down the center of the paper and on the left side you would write the reasons why the customer should buy the vacuum, and on the right side the reasons they shouldn't. It was apparently named after Benjamin Franklin, who was one of our founding fathers, and who sometimes argued with Alexander Hamilton, and other times argued against slavery, but only after it had fallen out of style.

Our company had taught us that before deploying this particular strategy with a customer that we should be certain that the pros would outweigh the cons, and while I couldn't say for certain that the guilty column would easily outweigh the not-guilty column, what I did know is that this sort of list would likely assist everyone in coming to a fair and just verdict, so that is what we agreed to do.

I drew a line down the center of a fresh sheet of paper, and on the left I wrote Guilty and on the right I wrote Not-Guilty. Then I added in what we had talked about so far, so it ended up looking like this:

Guilty	Not-Guilty
Crooks must have had murder weapon in his hand when he confronted Mrs. Baker, because he was stealing it	Crooks may not have stolen it because it was heavy. So maybe husband brought it from downstairs
Burglars would have silenced the witness upon being discovered	They would have just left rather than commit murder
Extreme coincidence burglars chose to rob home where a murder had just taken place	Coincidences happen
Husband had no clear motive to kill his wife	Husband may have been abusive and killed her in a fit of rage long coming

Thus far, the two sides stacked up fairly evenly, and while such an even calculation may have been frowned upon by my company when trying to sell vacuums, I believed that it was responsibly applied in the present situation, where we were trying to decide if the state had proven its case beyond a reasonable doubt.

"I know many men are abusive to their partners. Lord knows I see it. But I also think it would be rather craven of him to murder his wife and then go directly to a business meeting. I mean, unless he is an absolute monster."

It was the nurse who'd said it, and while she was probably correct in most circumstances, I couldn't help thinking of the times that I had committed murder, and then immediately chopped up the body and gone out to dinner, or on a date, or spent time with my family. In this way, I wondered if maybe I was a monster to be able to do these things and act that way, and even if I wasn't a full-on monster like Godzilla or Dracula, that maybe there was enough monster in me to qualify for that label.

I might have gone on thinking about it much longer if my thoughts hadn't been interrupted by the garbage collector/relocator, who stepped into the conversation rather fiercely and suddenly, so as it turns out I didn't have to think about what kind of monster I was for very long.

Chapter 8

Is everyone forgetting that Mr. Crooks's DNA was found on the body?"

This wasn't quite accurate, since his DNA was actually found just a few feet away from Mrs. Baker's body, as several people were quick to point out. However, his point was well taken. In fact, the two most damning pieces of evidence against Mr. Crooks were likely Mr. Crooks's hair found three feet from the body, and what Mr. Munroe had testified to, about Crooks admitting to assaulting her.

For Mr. Crooks not to have been the killer, there must be an innocent explanation for one of his hairs being so close to the body, and Mr. Munroe must also be lying about Mr. Crooks' confession to him in the van.

The discussion started with the hair. Everyone agreed that Crooks must have been in the room, which was easy to conclude, since Mr. Crooks himself had admitted to being there.

"He just said that because he had to," said juror number four. "Bet your ass if they hadn't found the hair on the floor, he would have said he'd never stepped foot inside. I know these people. They just say what they have to."

While I generally didn't like to agree with juror number four, and while I didn't exactly understand what he meant by "these people", the fact was that he made a good point.

Since his hair was found near the body, it would have been foolhardy to take a contrary position to having been in the bedroom. So we all agreed quickly that he had been in the bedroom, and thus his admission of same meant very little.

"If it was just the hair," said the CEO, "given the young lady's concerns, that alone might not be enough. But we also have Mr. Munroe's testimony, that his friend had admitted to striking her."

I saw the accountant thumbing through his notes, and then he said, reading aloud directly from a page, "I wrote it down, that 'he knocked her the fuck out.'"

"That's what I have, too," said the nurse, and then several others nodded in agreement.

"So then the question is, do we believe Mr. Munroe, at least, on that point?" asked the baker.

We debated whether or not Mr. Munroe would have a motive to lie about that particular point, and while most of us agreed that he would not, there were several who had a doubt.

"I wouldn't believe a word that comes out of their mouths," said juror number four.

"But he could have lied to help his friend in any number of ways," said the nurse. "I mean, he could have lied in a way that exonerated them both."

"You're assuming he'd want to lie to help his friend," said Shelley's sister. "Maybe by pointing the finger at his friend it would both seal the murder against Mr. Crooks while also demonstrating that he only heard about it in the car when they were leaving."

Shelley's sister was suggesting that perhaps Mr. Munroe's statement was a calculated one to insulate himself from culpability, because if we accepted that the statement was made, then we would likely have to accept the circumstances in which it was made, which was only in the getaway vehicle as they were leaving the scene.

"Is he possibly that cunning?" said the Adventurer.

We debated these points for the next hour, pausing only for dinner, then continued into the evening. It was only then that the baker brought up the fact that Mr. Crooks had called Mr. Munroe "a rat" in the courtroom.

While I had never had a pet rat, I did think that they were cute, largely misunderstood animals that were deserving of life just like the rest of us. Only most people didn't seem to agree and made a concerted effort to eradicate them from existence, except when they appeared in cartoon form in a television show or a movie.

For some reason, the term rat was used to signify a dishonorable or treacherous person, which I found to be both unfair and inaccurate, as it wasn't vermin who committed burglary or rape or murder, but people themselves, and I had never heard of a rat breaking into a person's mansion, except maybe to come in from the cold and find a bit of cheese, and certainly never to steal someone's marble bookends.

"Actually, I think he called him 'a fucking rat'," said the CEO, and most of the jurors agreed.

"Point is," added the baker, "you don't refer to someone as a rat when they are lying. You refer to someone that way when they betray you to the authorities by telling the truth."

I believed that the baker was correct, as criminal informants were sometimes also referred to as rats, because they covertly provided information to the police about crimes.

"I do believe it is significant," I said, "that he used that particular phrase."

"He could have just called him a liar," said the nurse. "But he didn't."

We spoke a bit longer about the rat outburst, and then finally I updated my chart for The Benjamin Franklin

Close, listing out all of the options for guilt or innocence of Mr. Crooks.

Guilty	Not-Guilty
Crooks must have had murder weapon in his hand when he confronted Mrs. Baker, because he was stealing it	Crooks may not have stolen it because it was heavy. So maybe husband brought it from downstairs
Burglars would have silenced the witness upon being discovered	They would have just left rather than commit murder
Extreme coincidence burglars chose to rob home where a murder had just taken place	Coincidences happen
Husband had no clear motive to kill his wife	Husband may have been abusive and killed her in a fit of rage long coming
DNA found by body, meaning he was there	He might have just walked into the room
Admission to Mr. Munroe (for Crooks)	Munroe possible lying
Calling Mr. Munroe "a rat" meant he exposed what Crooks actually said	Poor choice of words through emotion

At this point, I slid my notepad over to Shelley's sister, and I could see her hemming and hawing over the list, only by then I was more confident than ever that Mr. Crooks had committed the murder, and I couldn't imagine any contrary verdict. That was when I remembered The Imaginary Close, which was a strategy we would use by inviting the customer to imagine a situation in the event they did not purchase the vacuum, and the suggestion was always supposed to be an unpleasant one. So we would say, "imagine you do not purchase this vacuum now, and then they are sold out later," or, "imagine that you continue using your old vacuum, and it leaves 25% more dust motes in the carpet, and your dog sniffs them and dies." Unfortunately, many people didn't have much of an imagination, and it would turn out that the only thing they could truly imagine in that moment was to quickly get off the telephone and go about their daily business. Only occasionally it did work, and the person would say, "well, I wouldn't want that," and then start providing their credit card information, and even if the success rate was only a small one, I figured that it might work in tandem with The Benjamin Franklin Close, so as Shelley's sister was looking at the list, I said, "Imagine if we do not find Mr. Crooks guilty, in light of all this evidence against him?"

It only took another minute, but soon enough she had mouthed the word "Guilty," and we were all done with Mr. Crooks, even if he didn't know it.

I updated my verdict sheet, which now looked like this:

Peter Crooks:	**Guilty**	**Not-Guilty**
Burglary	12	0
Murder	12	0

Sheldon Munroe:	**Guilty**	**Not-Guilty**
Burglary	12	0
Murder	6	6
Accessory after the fact to murder	10	2
Cruelty to animals	11	1

This left only Mr. Munroe's charges to resolve, but by then it was nearly nine o'clock, and everyone seemed rather tired, so we decided to break until Wednesday morning.

This meant a second night at the hotel, and while part of me just wanted to be done with this and get back home to my family, it was an important decision to be made, and I knew that it would be irresponsible to rush through it. What's more, I recognized that there was still a part of me that was drawn to Shelley's sister, and since there was a chance we could reach our verdict tomorrow, I felt that I best sort that part out one way or the other tonight, so that is what I decided to do.

Chapter 9

It was 9:30 p.m. by the time we got back to the hotel.

I had asked for a beer to be sent to my room just as I had the night before, then I took a shower and stepped into the hallway, where I was met by Nancy, who was seated in a chair halfway down the hallway.

"Help you out, sir?"

"I would just like to speak with juror number five."

"Is she expecting you?"

I couldn't answer this with any certainty because I didn't know what was in her mind, but I did say, "We do not have an appointment," which seemed to adequately answer her question, even if she did look at me strangely after I'd said it.

Finally, she said, "Come with me," then escorted me to room #13, even though I already knew that was her room because I had taken note of it the night we'd arrived. I had also noted that juror number four was in room #9, just a few doors down.

Nancy knocked on the door, and a few moments later it opened.

"You have a visitor," she said, but remained standing beside us, presumably waiting to hear what Shelley's sister had to say about it.

"I was hoping to speak with you if it is not too late."

She lolled about the door for a moment before saying, "Sure," then retreated back inside her room, allowing me to follow her inside, while Nancy closed the door quietly behind us.

"So, what's up?"

She sat down on her bed and crossed her legs while I took a seat in a nearby chair. She was wearing tight leggings and a plain white t-shirt. I couldn't say for sure why I had gone there that night, only that I felt things between us were unsettled. Finally, I said, "I would like to speak with you about recent events."

"Recent events, huh?"

I wasn't sure how to begin because there were many things I wanted to say.

"I did not like siding with him against you."

She just shrugged when I said it, only she looked down briefly as she did.

"He does not seem to like it when you speak, especially if you have something to say that is against his views."

"I think a lot of men want women to still act like girls."

I didn't know exactly what she meant by that, but I didn't ask her to clarify. Then I remembered how The Imaginary Close seemed to work well enough on her to cause her to vote for life imprisonment for a man, so if it worked that well I thought that it might work again if she hadn't already caught onto it.

"Imagine if I was to change my vote, simply to side with your position?"

She became quiet after I said it, and then looked down toward her knees, which she'd brought up close to her chin.

"Yeah, I understand. I wouldn't want you to do that."

"I do believe that he is guilty."

"I know you do, and so do I. But that husband…"

Her voice trailed off then and she didn't complete her sentence, unless that was all she'd actually wanted to say, which in that case would have meant that she had.

We were both quiet after that, and when she looked up again from her knees she just stared into my eyes, so I thought this was as good a time as any to say some of the other things that had been in my head.

"I have been thinking about you," I said. I said it because it was true.

"Have you, now?" She had a bit of a smile on her face when she said it.

"I have. But I have not felt good about it, because I live with Donna, and we have a son together, and a dog and a cat."

She did not seem particularly fazed by any of this.

"When you invited me to come watch you dance, I had contemplated coming, but I was sick. Only then I had a dream about you that night, a dream so real that I thought it had actually happened."

"And what did we do in this dream?" she asked, and the smile seemed to grow larger.

I told her that she had helped me to achieve it twice in her dressing room. She smiled when I said it, and even let out a slight laugh, though I suppose it might have been just a giggle.

"So, is this a confession, or an invitation, or what exactly?"

"I just wanted to tell you about it, and that if I have been behaving strangely toward you, I thought that this might help to explain it."

She didn't seem to know how to respond to this, so I responded to it myself.

"Do you believe that it is cheating if you cheat on someone with your mind?"

She thought about it for a few seconds before answering.

"Some people do. But I think if that's the case then everyone in the world is a cheater. You can't help but think about other people from time to time. Especially in dreams."

"I suppose that is true."

She was still smiling at me from her position on the bed.

"I do not wish to cheat on Donna," I said.

She stared at me for a bit before finally speaking.

"You're a real different guy, aren't you?"

I had been called many things before, and being different was certainly one of them. However, she hadn't said it in a mean or pejorative way like many others did.

"I suppose so," I said, only I left off the part about how different I really was because there were aspects about my past behavior that I felt it best not to share with anyone. And even though we were in the throes of brutal honesty, experience had taught me that sometimes there was a thing as too much honesty, and this was probably one of those times.

She then turned very quiet, and as I looked at her I couldn't help but think about how pretty she was, and how I would very much like to achieve it with her, even though Nancy was seated outside the door just twenty feet away. Only I already knew that it would not be proper, and I believed that she knew it too, and that was when I finally got up from my chair.

"Leaving so soon?"

I said that I'd better, since we had to be up early to continue our deliberations. This was the truth, of course, but it was only half of the truth. The fact was that I was not only drawn to her because she was an attractive woman, but because there was a kindness in her that I found very attractive. And I felt that I'd best leave quickly since I had said what needed to be said, and before I gave into temptation.

I started for the door, and she was soon on her feet right behind me, so I turned to face her.

"I believe that if I were not with Donna, I would be very happy to be with someone like you."

She just tilted her head and looked at me with her eyes moist, and it seemed like she was going to cry.

"I am sorry if this exchange has tarnished our relationship."

She didn't say anything else, though she did come forward and take me in her arms in something of a hug, kissing me softly on the cheek as she did.

When I finally emerged back into the hallway, I not only saw Nancy seated with her book, but I also saw juror number four walking down the hallway holding an ice bucket, which he must have just recently filled. He stopped when he saw me, and he must have known whose room I was exiting because he immediately got a funny look on his face and then smirked as if he'd caught me in the act of doing something improper. Then he said, "Sleep tight, Melville," in a rather mocking fashion before stepping back inside his room.

His door had only just closed when I felt some of my scary thoughts returning, and I couldn't help thinking about how he had just tarnished what was an otherwise tender and decent moment. And I started thinking about the things I might have done to him if we were alone, and how much I wanted to finish what I'd achieved in my medicine induced haze. Only then just as quickly as I'd started thinking those thoughts, I thought about what the custodian had told me, and how if it were him, he would keep things civilized, and then settle up on the outside.

Keep things civil. Then settle up on the outside.

Of course, he was just the custodian.

Chapter 10

I felt much better about things with Shelley's sister when I saw her again the next morning, and I could tell that she must have felt the same because she gave me a warm smile when she saw me at breakfast, which was served for us in the hotel restaurant.

The retired police officer, on the other hand, remained rude and obnoxious. He was loud again during breakfast, and he started saying that if we'd listened to him sooner, we'd all be home tucked in bed with our families, as if we were to blame for how long the process was taking.

When we finally got back to the courthouse, we commenced debating Mr. Munroe's murder charge. However, unlike our deliberations about Mr. Crooks the day before, this particular deliberation took surprisingly little time once we reasoned that since we had accepted Mr. Munroe's testimony about what Mr. Crooks had divulged to him in the truck, it must have meant that he only found about the murder after it happened. As such, the six people who had originally voted that he was guilty, slowly but surely came around to the conclusion that given their acceptance of his testimony in convicting Mr. Crooks, they had no choice but to conclude that the news about Mr. Crooks's attack must have taken Mr. Munroe by surprise in the car, meaning that he had neither been involved in the attack nor was he aware it was going to happen. If nothing else, they accepted that there must at least be a reasonable doubt, and as the judge had told us, that was enough to find him not guilty.

Juror number four was the last holdout, but even he finally relented, and finally he voted not guilty, only not before saying, "If you all want someone like that walking around your streets, who am I to say no?" which was his way of saying that he was only voting this way because the rest of us were.

As a result, Mr. Munroe's verdict sheet now looked like this:

Sheldon Munroe:	**Guilty**	**Not-Guilty**
Burglary	12	0
Murder	0	12
Accessory after the fact to murder	10	2
Cruelty to animals	1	11

This left only two charges for Mr. Munroe, the accessory after the fact to murder, and the cruelty to animals charge, or in this case a single animal, the dog Herbert.

The accessory after the fact to murder involved whether we were convinced beyond a reasonable doubt that Mr. Munroe aided or abetted Mr. Crooks following the murder, and since he had driven them away from the scene after Mr. Crooks had told him what he had done, the only real question was whether or not he knew that he was helping Mr. Crooks to escape a murder scene.

Only the nurse and the baker had voted not guilty. Their view was that even though Mr. Crooks had told Mr. Munroe that he had, "knocked her the fuck out," that this didn't necessarily mean that he had killed her. And since Mr. Munroe was not charged with aiding and abetting an assault, but a murder, that it was impossible to find him guilty of that offence given his limited knowledge of what had actually taken place in the bedroom at the time he had driven them both away.

This resulted in a lively debate. In fact, after the nurse and the baker had each been afforded an opportunity to state their case for a vote of not guilty, four others quickly agreed with them, myself included, which rendered the vote 6-6. The plumber had actually been one of the first to come around, which was a bit surprising given what he had said to me when we were first sequestered, and when he seemed rather convinced of their guilt. He realized that since Mr. Munroe was the driver and was tasked with driving away from the scene regardless, then it would be impossible to find beyond a reasonable doubt that the purpose of him driving away was to aid and abet the sudden murder, rather than just driving away as previously planned. I saw a lot of people nodding along when he said all this, and only realized after a moment that one of the heads bobbing up and down was my own.

It was only after we'd eaten lunch and had made no further progress, that we agreed to table that discussion and turn to the last remaining count, the cruelty to animals.

Up to this point I had tried my best to remain objective about this charge and to judge Mr. Munroe fairly on all of the other counts he was facing. However, as we began to review the evidence relevant to this charge, I could feel my mood starting to change.

Herbert had been found locked in a room on the ground floor, and Mr. Munroe's thumbprint had been found on the doorknob. Herbert had been treated for some cracked ribs and one of his teeth had been knocked out. Photographs of Herbert had been made exhibits, and the nurse had just now spread them across the table.

As I looked at the photographs, I couldn't help but dwell on one particular image. It showed a close-up of Herbert's face, his lips and gums red and swollen where the tooth had been knocked out, and his eyes looking watery and sad. I became angrier and angrier as I looked at it, and finally I excused myself from the table and walked over to the water cooler to have a drink. It wasn't long before Shelley's sister stood up and came over to where I was standing.

"Are you ok?"

I wasn't sure how to express what I was feeling, so I just said, "It's important to stay hydrated," which, although not completely responsive to her inquiry, was at least not a lie, based on what I had read in some health magazines.

"I guess you're right about that," she said.

I filled up the cup for a second time, and after I had consumed its contents, I felt her hand on my arm, only she didn't say anything. This was her way of saying that she was here for me, but that we didn't have to talk, and I appreciated both of these things very much. I then took a moment to look out the window. She remained by my side the whole time, and after another minute we both returned to the table, at which point the student, who was the sole vote of not-guilty on the animal abuse charge, was called upon to articulate her doubts.

"The only thing we have tying this guy to the dog is the fingerprint on the door handle," she said.

"Isn't that enough?" said the CEO to my left. "Doesn't get much better than that, does it?"

"But you heard what the police said. There were other fingerprints on the door, including both Mr. and Mrs. Baker, and several other prints from unknown persons."

"So, you think maybe Mrs. Baker beat up her own dog before she was killed?"

This was juror number four, who, as always, delivered his comment in a rather condescending tone.

"Look, you're the one who said the husband was abusive," she said, looking at Shelley's sister. "How do we know if it wasn't him? Or someone else? Or even if it wasn't an accident?"

"That seems like speculation," said the nurse. "Sure, it could be any of those things, but I think if we apply common sense and consider the context in which the dog was found, it seems very likely that the dog was attacked by the intruders."

"But is 'very likely' enough?" asked the student, standing her ground.

"In this case, I believe it is," said the baker, and many others agreed.

I had been listening to the student's concerns, and as I did I cycled through some of the closing techniques that might apply to the current predicament. I also decided to avoid techniques that I had already used because I had recently seen a news report that said we use too many antibiotics in our food, and because we get exposed to them so often it decreases their potency, and while I couldn't say that repeated use of the company closing techniques would result in the same loss of potency as repeated exposure to antibiotics, I couldn't be sure of it, so I decided to err on the side of caution.

I decided to begin with The Apology Close, so I said, "I'm sorry, the fault must be ours if we have been unable to convince you of the matter."

She just looked at me and nodded, only then juror number four said, "How 'bout you speak for yourself, eh, Mac?" which was his way of saying that he did not wish to apologize and that I should not speak for him, so, as it turned out, The Apology Close worked better when you were speaking for yourself rather than in a room full of other people.

I then immediately shifted into The Sharp Angle Close.

"If I can convince you that Mr. Munroe struck the dog, would that change your vote?"

"Of course," she said.

The Sharp Angle Close involved a "sharp" identification of the customer's main objection, followed by a promise to satisfy that concern. For example, if a customer said that they could only afford $400 for a vacuum, we might offer a reduction in price to $400 if they were to purchase it that day. Unfortunately, I had started into The Sharp Angle Close without knowing precisely how to finish it, but I muddled ahead as best I could.

"Do you agree that he must have placed his hand on the door where the dog was found?"

She agreed that this must have happened, and that she had no reason to disbelieve the police evidence on this point.

"And do you agree that one places their hand on a door in order to open it?"

Again she agreed, which seemed very reasonable.

"And do you agree that if a person opens a door, it is likely the dog would run out, unless held back or beaten back by force?"

At this point she did not agree, because she said the dog could just be pushed back and the door closed, without having to use much force.

Like many of these closing strategies, it turns out that they work better for selling vacuums than in convincing jurors to find people guilty of crimes, and so despite my best efforts, I decided that I could not outsmart the student.

I had found previously that the effectiveness of the sales closing techniques was inversely effective with the age of the person, and as she was by far the youngest of the jurors, this stayed true to form. Perhaps the starkest example was the time that I had tried to implement The Compromise Close with Toby, offering him a cupcake if he were only to finish half of his dinner. He had responded by simply sticking his finger in his nose, which suggested either some level of immunity from such psychological trickery, or some inexplicable aversion to small baked treats.

We debated with the student for nearly another hour, stopping only mid-afternoon for a coffee break, as people grew increasingly frustrated with the student, myself included. That's when I took my cup over to the window where there were a few chairs set against the wall, and where the old woman was seated with a cup of tea.

"How are you doing, young man?"

I told her that I was fine, but that I was tired. I felt this response was true in two respects, not only physically, having only recently recovered from being sick, but also emotionally, given the many difficult thoughts and decisions that my brain had been forced to navigate.

"I think we're all a little tired," she said, adding, "I just hope we get through it today so I can go back home to my Daisy."

"I am not confident that we will reach a consensus on these last two counts."

"Well, they can't make us stay in here forever."

I hadn't actually considered this, and I wondered if she was correct about it. "I would like to return home to my family, as well."

She smiled and patted my hand when I said it.

"My husband, God rest his soul, he once spent a full week deliberating on a jury trial. I just couldn't imagine being gone that long from my Daisy."

I could feel the concern in her voice when she said her dog's name, and then I started thinking about Molly, and how it would be awful to be an animal and not understand why your master had gone away. That got me thinking about some other things, and that's when I got to me feet and walked over to the table where I again looked at the photographs of Herbert. Only this time I looked at them differently, which was to say that I looked at them in a way that I hadn't considered before, and then I started thinking about other things, and then finally I thought about the custodian, and I had only just started thinking about the custodian when the accountant called us all back to the table.

To my surprise, we had only just sat down when the student said that she would like to change her vote on the animal cruelty charge from not guilty to guilty. She had apparently been in discussion with both the Adventurer and the dentist over the break, and they had convinced her that the chances of another person hurting the dog would be so far-fetched in the circumstances that any doubt would not be a reasonable one.

"Halle-fucking-lujah," said juror number four, and though none of the others expressed themselves so crudely, I saw several other looks of relief on my fellow jurors' faces.

"So," said the Accountant, "now that that's finished, we just have to settle up the accessory count."

This was when I raised my hand.

"Juror number nine," he said, "you have something to add?"

"I do," I said, as the room turned quickly silent. "I would like to change my vote on the animal cruelty charge to not guilty."

I said it because it was true.

Chapter 11

My decision was not received well.

I could immediately sense everyone's eyes on me, which was rather uncomfortable, but perhaps understand-able in the circumstances.

"Well, ain't he a peach?"

This was juror number four, and while I would normally have taken offence at his making yet another condescending comment, and perhaps already be envisioning some dramatic and gruesome way to open up one of his arteries over the jury room table, the fact was that my thoughts were sufficiently preoccupied with other thoughts in such a way that there apparently wasn't enough room for the scary ones.

"Well, sir," said the accountant, who remained quite professional despite this sudden turn of events, and which I felt reflected well on a jury foreman, and likely validated our selection of him for the position, "would you care to enlighten us on why the change?"

I knew that they would likely want to know, and surely deserved at least some explanation for my sudden reversal. However, I equally knew that there was no way that I would be able to explain my reasoning with any semblance of understanding.

"I would rather not," I said.

"Get this fucking guy," said juror number four, only I could tell that he was exceptionally frustrated by the way he said it, and I couldn't help taking some small amount of satisfaction from this.

"We have just been debating this for more than two hours," said the baker. "Surely you owe us some level of explanation?"

"Yes, I probably do," I conceded. "But I choose not to."

I saw some other looks of exasperation on the faces of my fellow jurors, including a noticeable grimace on the Adventurer, who had until then always served as the peacemaker, at least when he wasn't fighting kangaroos who might have had joeys in their pouches.

This was when juror number four rose to his feet.

"You're going to fucking explain yourself," he said, and I could tell by his tone and by how his face had reddened that he was exceptionally angry.

"No, I do not believe that I will," I said, and there was something about his histrionic manner that made it much easier for me to remain calm as I said it, and to be quite satisfied in doing so.

This was when the CEO suggested, "Why don't we take another break," and so we did, and while several people approached me to discuss the matter, I had by then quite settled on my position.

Following this second break, the jurors attempted to reason with me, either to change my vote back to guilty, or at least to explain my reservations, but I held firm in my positions on both, and they quickly realized it was hopeless. As a result, they reluctantly accepted this reality, and this resulted in the following tabulations:

Sheldon Munroe:	**Guilty**	**Not-Guilty**
Burglary	12	0
Murder	0	12
Accessory after the fact to murder	6	6
Cruelty to animals	11	1

We had briefly gone back to the accessory count, but with the vote split 6-6, and each camp rather settled in their positions, it was agreed that we were at an impasse. I believe that people had also reached the end of their patience, so we advised our jury attendant that we had deliberated for as long as we could.

It was shortly before dinner when we were all called back into the courtroom with the judge, the lawyers, and the defendants.

"I understand that you have reached a verdict on two of the counts, but are unable to reach a verdict on two others?"

We nodded when the judge said it, only some only did so while also glaring in my direction.

"I must ask that you explore every possible avenue to reconcile your differences and to reach a unanimous verdict," she said, adding, "A hung jury on any of the counts means that the state may be required to re-litigate those charges."

Again we nodded when she said it, and after another stern admonition to do our best to reach a consensus, we were sent back into the jury room to continue our deliberations.

Given the hour, we ordered food and took dinner in the jury room so everyone could cool off. Then, after another hour of futile discussions, we informed the jury attendant that nothing had changed, and thus we re-convened in the courtroom with all the parties present.

It was nearly eight o'clock when we stepped back into the courtroom. It was only then that I noticed how full the courtroom was, including Mr. Baker, and the media. In all there must have been nearly fifty people in the courtroom, in addition to the court staff and the defendants.

"I understand that you remain hung on two of the counts?" said the judge.

The accountant, acting as our foreperson, was already on his feet and answered in the affirmative.

"And that you are convinced that further deliberations will not assist?"

"Yes, Your Honor."

"Very well," she said through something of a frustrated tone, "if you could please submit your verdict sheet."

He provided it to the jury attendant, who submitted it to the court. The judge reviewed it silently to herself, then handed it back to the court registrar, who provided it to the jury attendant, who returned it to our foreperson.

The court registrar then read out each count.

"On the first count of burglary, as against Mr. Crooks, how does the jury find?"

"We find the defendant guilty."

I looked over at Mr. Crooks and his counsel, and neither of them reacted. Mr. Crooks's counsel had been smirking arrogantly since we'd entered the courtroom, and he remained so as the verdicts were read.

"On the first count of burglary, as against Mr. Munroe, how does the jury find?"

"We find the defendant guilty."

Neither Mr. Munroe nor his counsel reacted to this verdict, which was not unexpected, given that they themselves had invited the jury to make findings of guilt.

"On the second count of murder, as against Mr. Crooks, how does the jury find?"

"We find the defendant guilty."

To this, Mr. Crooks's lawyer scoffed and threw his pen into the air, at which point the judge yelled, "Order," and banged down her gavel. Mr. Crooks himself just shook his head, as if he were both surprised and disappointed in the result, but beyond that betrayed little emotion.

"On the second count of murder, as against Mr. Munroe, how does the jury find?"

"We find the defendant not guilty."

Mr. Munroe bent his head down in the prisoner's box, and moments later he began to weep, which I thought was poignant, given his nickname. I then saw him raise his head in our direction and mouth the words "Thank you." His lawyer still did not react.

"On the third count of accessory after the fact, as against Mr. Munroe, how does the jury find?"

"We are unable to reach a verdict."

"And on the fourth count of animal cruelty, as against Mr. Munroe, how does the jury find?"

"We are unable to reach a verdict."

With that, I watched as Mr. Munroe's counsel finally turned in his client's direction, and the two men nodded at one another. Mr. Crooks' lawyer remained seated shaking his head. Meanwhile, I saw many people in the gallery, who I presumed to be Mrs. Baker's family, to be hugging and crying, only nobody seemed to hug Mr. Baker. There was then a great murmur in the courtroom, and many flash bulbs all around from the media, until the judge smacked her gavel to return order.

"I want to thank the jury for their hard work and dedication," she said, adding, "You have performed a vitally importance service, and your community thanks you. You are excused."

With that she smacked her gavel once again, only unlike the previous times that she had done it, this one

somehow sounded sweeter because it meant we were
finally free.

Chapter 12

Many of us shook hands and hugged once back in the jury room, which seemed to be something that people liked to do, only I steered clear of juror number four, and it would appear that he also steered clear of me.

The old woman took both of my hands in her shaky ones and praised me on being such a good man and told me that I should be proud that I stood up for my principles. Then, after saying goodbye to several others, I walked out of the courthouse with Shelley's sister. We stopped out front on the sidewalk, where it was already dark out.

"Well, it's been a ride," she said.

"Yes."

"I'm really glad that I got to know you."

I felt the same way, then I said it.

"I can't wait to talk to Shelley about all this."

"And I believe I will discuss things with Donna," I said.

She didn't answer right away, and I saw a thoughtful look come onto her face.

"I hope things work out between you," she said.

This time she didn't invite me to the Rocksteady, but she did say, "I hope to see you again one day," which was a kind thing to say, even if it was unrealistic.

She hugged me again, and this time gave me a kiss on the opposite cheek from last night, which seemed like a nice way to bookend things.

Then I walked to my car and placed my suitcase in my trunk before turning my car on and driving home.

It was nearly nine o'clock when I pulled into the driveway, and Donna must have heard this because by the time I stepped inside she was standing in the foyer waiting to greet me.

"So, how do you feel?"

I had already sent Donna a message about the outcome. The fact was that I felt a great many things in that moment, but the feeling I felt strongest and most of all was that I felt good to finally be home. Then I said it.

Donna then took my suitcase out of my hands and carried it upstairs, and in that instant, I briefly questioned what I had done, and how I had freed Mr. Munroe of the animal cruelty charge, only just then I saw some of Toby's Legos sprinkled out along the floor, and I knew again that I had made the right decision.

❧❧❧

It was front-page news in the morning newspaper.

Both men had been sentenced shortly after we'd been excused. Mr. Crooks received a life sentence without the chance of parole, given the brutal nature of the crime and his former criminal history. His lawyer was quoted as saying, "I am very disappointed with the jury's decision. Frankly, I'm not sure they were watching the same trial that I was," which was something many lawyers liked to say even when they didn't actually believe it. Then he went on to say that they would be pursuing all avenues of appeal.

Mr. Munroe, on the other hand, had only been found guilty of the burglary charge, and since he had been in custody for the last eight months, he received time served and was released from custody that very night. The state would have to decide whether or not they wished to re-try him on the accessory to murder and the cruelty to animals since we did not reach a verdict on those charges, but until they did so he was a free man. When asked for comment on the front steps of the courthouse, he just said that he was thankful it was over and that he wanted to go for a burger.

Now that the whole affair had concluded, I couldn't help but reflect on how strange it was, and perhaps hypocritically, that I had been put in a position to judge other men for murder. However, I also recognized that I had been forced into servitude against my will, so there was little that could be done about it, and while the experience did provide me the opportunity to engage with other members of my community in a meaningful way in performing our civic duty, it had mostly just reminded me how much I disliked interacting with other people.

I had just finished reading the newspaper story when Toby came running downstairs and into the kitchen, where he hugged the side of my leg, then immediately started crying.

"I have missed you," I said as I patted the top of his head.

He said something in response, and while he was too sobby and sniffley for me to make any sense of it, I would like to believe that he reciprocated the sentiment.

I then told him I was home now for good and there was no need to cry, only then I thought about how I shouldn't suppress his emotions by suggesting it was something that he shouldn't do. I knew that some men told their boys not to cry because it wasn't manly, and even if Toby wasn't very manly at four years old, I did not want crying to have a negative connotation, so finally I said, "You may cry if you wish, son," only by then he'd already stopped, suggesting that perhaps he did not require my advice on this issue.

"Daddy," he said, after pulling back from me and wiping his sleeve across his face, "will you make me cereal?"

I had often found with children that they could vacillate between hopeless despondence to regular affability in mere seconds, and even if Donna herself could sometimes challenge Toby's level of psychological fluctuation, the fact was that I had yet to meet any being quite as unstable as an upset toddler.

I made him cereal as requested, which was to say that I simply shook some cereal into one of his favorite bowls and then poured milk overtop, but as Toby was easily impressed by simple tasks, he reacted as if this was a great feat, and so in my mind I decided to treat it as such.

Then he said, "I missed you, Daddy," as he slurped up a spoonful, so I told him that I missed him, too. And it was easy to say, given that I felt it quite strongly.

That was when Donna entered the kitchen wearing her bathrobe. I presumed that she was not wearing anything underneath because she had been quite naked when I got out of bed that morning, and while I sometimes questioned if this was appropriate attire so close to our son, I figured that since he owed his entire existence to his mother's body, he probably shouldn't get too fussed about what she did with it.

We then spent a happy day together as a family, including two hours at a nearby park, where Molly rolled around in clumps of multicolored leaves. And while my family and dog played and smiled and laughed, I couldn't help thinking about Mrs. Baker in that moment, and how she would never play with her family, or smile, or laugh ever again. And I had just started thinking about Herbert, and the photograph of his bloodied mouth with the puffed gums, when I pushed all these thoughts out of my head, which just made space for a whole series of new ones.

⁂

I returned to work on Monday and found Gordon seated at his desk ahead of me just as usual, only not before dropping off a box of donuts in the staff lunch room for my colleagues, and while I had said "Time to make the donuts" just as the baker had liked to say each morning he'd entered the jury room, they just looked at me strangely after I said it, so I quickly walked away.

"The prodigal son returns," said Gordon as I approached my desk and sat down beside him.

"How did you know it was me?" I asked.

"Oh, you got a certain walk," he said, turning in my direction. "Kind of slow and uptight."

"I see."

"I can usually tell who's coming, based on the sound of their walk or their smell or their general outline."

Gordon was not all the way blind but was just legally blind, which meant that he was sufficiently blind to be considered blind by our government, but not so blind that he couldn't still make out certain shapes and colors.

He'd apparently compensated for his lack of vision by acquiring a heightened senses of smell and hearing, which made me think about some of the superheroes that I used to read about in the comics, only in Gordon's case he hadn't been bitten by a radioactive spider or hit by gamma rays or come from a different planet. I suppose if he had then he might have been doing other things with his time than selling vacuums, though I suppose even a superhero could choose to sell vacuums if they really wanted to.

"You blank out again?"

Gordon had a way about being direct with me that most people didn't, and I found it both refreshing and frustrating.

"I was just thinking about some things," I said, and I felt this was largely accurate, even if the things I was thinking about was how Gordon compared weakly to some of the superheroes I'd read about in comics.

"Anyway, it's good to have you back. We've missed you around the house."

While I was happy to be back at my own home, with my own child and pets and wife, it still felt good to hear it.

"I am very grateful for your hospitality," I said.

"Yeah, well, don't get too broken up about it," he said, then turned back to his special keypad and started clicking in some numbers.

Gordon had an abrupt way about him where I never quite knew if he was offended by something I'd said or, like me, he just didn't enjoy wasting time on platitudes.

"Have you had much success in your sales?" I asked, hoping to move the conversation forward.

"Shit, I sold three Cyclones yesterday, to a place that doesn't even have carpet!"

The Cyclone was one of our newest model carpet cleaners. It was named after a type of weather event that produced a large spiral air mass and sometimes destroyed people's homes and communities. Our company often selected vacuum names that related closely to catastrophic weather events, and while I'd once questioned if this was a good idea, we were told that the names conjured up images of great power, which is what people liked and what caused them to spend their money, even if they didn't need to, only they left that last part unsaid. Still, for a while I wondered if we might be alienating some of our customers by likening our products to deadly weather systems, but then I also figured just as quickly that anyone who'd just lost their home in a major weather event probably wouldn't be out shopping for vacuums or carpet cleaners, so perhaps there was nothing to get too fussed about.

By then, I was also thinking about what Gordon had said about selling three Cyclones to a place that doesn't have carpet, especially since it was first and foremost a wet-dry carpet cleaner, and while I had found that Gordon had a unique ability to deploy the company sales strategies to sell our products, I couldn't help but wonder how he was able to sell carpet cleaners to a company that didn't actually have any carpet.

"I told 'em it would clean their door mats and yoga mats and some other bullshit."

"I see."

"Who wants to pay to clean that stuff when you can have a Cyclone and clean 'em yourself?"

While I considered Gordon my friend, I had also found him to be rather unscrupulous when it came to selling our vacuums and other products, and while it is possible that the purchase of the Cyclones might be a wise investment for that company to clean their door mats, I felt that it was much more likely that spending a thousand dollars on each unit would be a tremendous waste of money.

I had just decided to drop the issue when Mr. Peters came up in between us.

"So, back from jury duty?" he asked. He said it as if it was a genuine question even though he could clearly see that I was sitting right in front of him, but I answered him nonetheless given that he was my boss, and it was best to keep your bosses happy by responding to them when they asked pointed questions.

"Well, it's good to have you back. Poor Gordon here's been carrying the load."

He slapped his hand down on Gordon's shoulder as he said it, and I could see that Gordon didn't appreciate the gesture all that much because I saw him grimace when it happened.

"I am pleased to be back," I said. I said it because it was true.

"Well, I better let you get caught up on things. But you come find me later, and you tell me all about that case."

I didn't respond to that as he walked away smiling, which was good, because I liked to lie to people as little as possible, and I had no intention of visiting with Mr. Peters to discuss the case. Not only did I not want to re-live the experience so soon, but I also didn't much like talking to my bosses unless it was absolutely necessary. In my experience, most people didn't much like spending time with their bosses, and I couldn't imagine that spending time with him talking about cold-blooded murder and animal abuse would have been tangibly more satisfying.

"That guy is such an asshole," said Gordon without looking up from his computer.

I turned to look and saw Mr. Peters far enough away that it seemed like he hadn't heard what Gordon had said, and I couldn't help think that Gordon was taking an awful chance by saying it as loudly as he had. Only then I remembered how he'd heard me coming, and maybe he could tell how far away I was with his extra senses, and I thought how maybe if Gordon didn't have abilities like the heroes I'd read about in comics, he at least had the ability to gauge when it was safe to call the boss an asshole, so maybe he didn't compare to them as weakly as I'd first imagined.

Chapter 13

Things had mostly returned to normal since I got back from jury duty.

We'd had Halloween nearly the day I had returned. Toby had wanted to be a witch for Halloween, and rather than correcting him by suggesting he ought to be a warlock because he was a boy, we just helped him pick out a small broom and painted his face green and we even found a treat bag that was shaped liked a cauldron, and while at first I didn't feel comfortable about Toby dressing up in a traditionally female costume, I had read an article in that month's issue of the child psychology magazine called "Gender Reveal" that said children grow up healthier and more open-minded when their parents don't impose stereotypical gender roles on them, so I decided against reinforcing the warlock.

The name of the article came from a recent ritual where attention-seeking couples would try to upstage one another in showy exhibitions to announce the gender of their children. When Toby was born we didn't do anything like that, which suited me fine because I generally liked to draw as little attention to myself as possible, and also because we figured that if our family or friends truly wanted to know what genitalia Toby had been born with, they would probably just ask.

Once we'd got Molly on her leash, our first stop was our next-door neighbor Hayley's house. This was the neighbor with whom Donna had previously believed I had performed a different sort of gender reveal.

"Trick or treat!" yelled Toby, as Hayley opened the door.

"Wow, are you a witch?" she said. Her dog Mister Muggles had wriggled up beside her and had started communicating with Molly as dogs sometimes do, by touching their noses together and wagging their tails.

Toby nodded up and down.

"Well then, I better give you some candy before you cast a spell on me!"

She placed some chocolate in Toby's plastic cauldron. Then we thanked her, and she smiled at me, but by then another child was already walking up the driveway, so that gave us a good reason to move along to the next house.

I hadn't spoken to Hayley since Donna had first banished me. I believe we had both purposely kept our distance given Donna's recent, unsubstantiated concerns about infidelity, and given what I had just gone through with Shelley's sister, I figured it would be best to distance myself from any women who weren't Donna.

As we moved on from house to house, I kept back on the sidewalk with Molly as Donna and Toby went up and knocked on the doors, and I remember how mostly I was thinking about the trial, given that it was so fresh in my mind, and about some of the injustices I had observed, and then I started thinking about what the custodian had told me in a rather self-deprecating fashion as he held his mop, and as we moved on around our block I could already feel myself holding Molly's leash tighter and tighter.

The fall air felt good against my face, and after a while I was able to detach myself from some of the thoughts that had started collecting in my head, and I do believe that it might have ended right there, without the need for more bloodshed, had I not worked with Gordon selling vacuums.

Chapter 14

I had only been home a few weeks when I brought a dog home for Toby.

"This will be your dog," I said, and Toby immediately hugged him tightly as Molly looked on suspiciously from the side.

Donna had her hands turned out at her sides.

"Uh, were you maybe going to run this by me?"

"I suppose I should have," I said, "only I wanted it to be a surprise."

"A surprise for Toby or a surprise for me?"

She did not seem very happy.

"I suppose a surprise for everyone," though it was really just a spontaneous decision I'd made in the moment a few days earlier.

"You know, we should really make large life decisions together."

I didn't get a chance to respond before Toby interrupted us. "What's his name, Daddy?"

I thought it over in my mind for a minute, and finally I suggested that maybe we could call him Herbert, and Toby seemed to be ok with this name, not only because he hadn't challenged me on the suggestion, but given the fact that he was already patting the top of the dog's head and calling him by that name. When I looked back up, I could see that Donna was still looking at me rather sternly.

"Anything else you want to tell me?"

"No," I said.

She looked at me curiously and shook her head, and I could tell that Donna was frustrated by my not including her in the decision-making process to acquire a new animal. Only I knew just as well that I couldn't fully explain it to her, at least not all the way explain it, lest I perhaps make Donna an accessory to a crime. So I figured that even if my explanation was sparse and imprecise, that it was still better than the potential for Toby to be raised without his parents, so I stood by my decision not to elaborate.

Molly and Herbert quickly became friends, and by the end of the day they were playing and barking at one another as if they had known each other their whole lives. They were also both instantly and unconditionally protective of Toby, which I had found to be an inherent trait of dogs, and what made them better than most humans.

Even Donna soon warmed up to him, though she still seemed unhappy with my decision not to consult her, given the way she was sitting rigid in bed and leafing aggressively through one of her beauty magazines. I had tried The Imaginary Close on her just before bed, saying, "Could you imagine if I had seen this nice dog for adoption and let the opportunity pass?" Only she responded just as quickly, "It could have waited a fucking hour," without turning her head, and while I'd briefly considered a segue into The Benjamin Franklin Close or The Sharp Angle Close or even something radical like The Follow The Leader Close, I quickly concluded that the best course of action might be to stop talking altogether, which was a strategy that I often used with Donna, and one that I had found was most effective with upset women.

The next morning I got up early and made everyone breakfast, and I promised Donna that I would make it up to her. This seemed to help, and she kissed me on the cheek before we set about our day, and it seemed as if the matter would soon be forgotten, at least until some unknown point in the future when she would surely bring it up again.

Chapter 15

When Donna had first asked me if there was anything else I wanted to tell her about acquiring Herbert, and I had said "No," it wasn't technically a lie because I hadn't actually "wanted" to share the other things in my mind. Had I done so, I believe that it would have been a very difficult discussion, and one that probably would have ended up with her clutching Toby securely and frantically calling 911 while perhaps extending a shakily held knife in my direction, and then later divorce and likely incarceration. So I was happy that she had phrased her question as she had.

However, had Donna simply meant to ask if there was more to the story, then my answer was not entirely the truth.

It had happened two nights ago.

Over the last week I'd been following him around and doing my best to learn some of his habits. It wasn't as hard as one would think, to find a person, and to follow them without their knowing if you knew just a little about them.

It was dark and rainy two nights ago, so I felt that I could follow him from a reasonably close distance without being noticed. He had entered into a vehicle after leaving work, and I followed it to a restaurant downtown where I could see through the glass window that he was meeting with a woman.

I remember how I'd parked across the road and turned all my lights off, and even if I didn't know precisely what I was going to do in that moment, I knew that I couldn't leave things as they were. So I waited, and I watched. And then finally, almost two hours later, he emerged from the restaurant with the woman. They kissed and parted ways on the sidewalk, and I watched as he got back into his car, and then I followed him home.

It was still dark and rainy as I watched him pull into his driveway and walk into the house. I then parked on one of the side streets and walked up to the front door, which he answered after I'd knocked.

"Hello," I said.

He started when he saw me, and I could see him squinting out into the darkness because he hadn't turned on the porch light.

"Yeah?"

I moved closer so he could better see my face, only I still didn't say anything.

"You?" he said as he recognized who I was. "Is there something I can help you with?"

"Yes," I said, "but it is a private matter. Perhaps we could speak inside?"

He invited me in, only he did so with some trepidation.

"What's this about?" he said, rather impatiently.

It looked very much as it did in the pictures. Only I didn't look for very long, because I did not want to be there any longer than I had to.

"I know what you did to Herbert."

"What the are you talking about?"

"I mean that I know that you beat him."

"This is about the fucking dog?"

I could see that he had a terrible temper, just as he had demonstrated in the courtroom.

"No," I said. "It is also about your wife."

"My wife?"

"You mistreated her," I said. I said it because it was true, only he became even angrier the moment I said it, and I could see he'd already clenched his fists.

"Where the fuck do you get off?" he said, only I wasn't dissuaded.

"I know that you beat her. And that you beat Herbert."

"Look fuck face, I was cleared."

"You hurt them both," I said, ignoring his last statement.

"I did, did I?"

"It is important that you demonstrate some remorse."

"Look, why don't you get the fuck out of my house?"

By then I had already reached into my pocket.

"Or better yet, how about we call the police, eh pal? And see what they have to say about this."

He had only just reached for his phone when I slid the knife into his throat. And as I did, I saw the blood draining out from the edges of the deep wound, and heard the gargling noises coming from his throat, and I couldn't help wondering about how none of this would have happened had Gordon's wife not worked at an animal shelter and had she not told Gordon, and had Gordon not told me. But he did tell me, and I went to visit the place where Herbert had been impounded. And I asked the shelter veterinarian about him, and she showed me his records, which had been sent over from his regular vet, because she wanted me to know about the injury history.

She'd said, "He's been through a lot, but he's a good little dog," which he certainly was. I had asked if I could have a copy of the records, and she said I could, but they would have to first redact any personal details of the people. So all the names and the private information were covered in big black strokes, but the substance of the records remained, including how one time the person who brought him in for treatment was a female with a black eye, and I thought this was a peculiar fact for the veterinarian to include, but I'm glad that she did, because as I watched Mr. Baker fall to the ground, wriggling at my feet and gasping for breath through all those red bubbles, I knew that he was a bad person, and that even if he didn't deserve all of what I'd just done to him, I felt that he probably deserved most of it.

Gordon's wife had heard about it from a friend at another shelter, and when she realized whose dog it was, she had told Gordon, and Gordon told me.

I was surprised that he'd been put up for adoption by Mr. Baker, and when I'd asked the veterinarian if there was a reason listed, it simply said, "Allergies." I'd then wondered aloud why he hadn't been left with Mrs. Baker's family, and she said that many times people drop off pets without consulting other family members, because they feel guilty or ashamed, or because they just don't care, and as I thought back on all of this, I concluded that he'd deserved not just most of it, but he'd also deserved the little bit left over as well.

But it wasn't just that he'd abandoned Herbert at a shelter, or how his wife had come in with a black eye. It was what the veterinarian had told me about the x-rays, and Herbert's injury history, and the amount of scar tissue, and how it was almost a certainty that the dog had been abused over a long period of time. That was when I knew that it was Mr. Baker who had beaten the dog and placed him in the room, and how he had also surely beaten Mrs. Baker before leaving for his meeting. Beaten her but not killed her. I was satisfied that that was indeed Mr. Crooks. But I still knew that I couldn't allow it.

When my fellow jurors had pressed me to explain why I'd changed my vote against Mr. Munroe on the animal cruelty charge, I knew that it would be hopeless to explain it. Only I knew that I was right about it. Right to change my vote suddenly as I had.

I remember speaking to the old woman by the window when we had taken a break from trying to convince the student, and I remember how she kept talking about her Daisy, and how she also mentioned her husband, only she didn't mention his name. And that got me thinking about the dentist, and how she talked about her dog Bandit and her two sons, but had never mentioned their names, and then Toby and his Lego police building, and how none of the people had names except for the dog, until I had prompted him to do so. And it got me thinking about how sincere I felt these people were, and how the only person in the trial who actually used Herbert's name spontaneously had been Mr. Munroe. It was all of that that had flashed into my mind as I'd stared out the window of the jury room while the other jurors were trying to convince the student, and just before I changed my own vote from guilty to not guilty. And even if it would have been impossible to explain, and even if it might not have made any sense to anyone else, I knew that it made a great deal of sense to me.

The animal shelter had required Herbert for another week for tests and quarantine before I could take him home, so it gave me time to do what I'd done.

Some people might say that it was premeditated because of how I tracked him down. Only this was only half-true, because I didn't know for sure that I was going to do what I did until I met him and spoke to him. So while it was somewhat premeditated, I wouldn't say that it was all the way premeditated.

All I knew in that moment was that I had to do it, so as he lay squirming at my feet, I murdered him in a most grievous and permanent way. Then I slipped out the side door where it was darker, and made my way back to my

car through small pockets of darkness before slipping
away into the night.

Chapter 16

I was two nine two five six seven."

"What's that?"

"That was my juror number."

It was the mustached police officer standing before me.

"There were eleven other jurors," I finally added.

"Yes, there were. Only none of them have been investigated for multiple suspicious deaths or disappearances."

I felt that this was a fair comment, only the fact of the matter was that these could all be explained away as unlikely coincidences, and while I knew they weren't just coincidences, I knew that the police couldn't be sure of it. That was likely why they'd invited me down there to speak that day, rather than arresting me and throwing me into the back of a paddy wagon, if they even still used those.

The police had called me that morning and asked if I would come in for questioning, so I took half a day off from work and went in after lunch to speak with them. I know that most lawyers would say that this was a bad idea, but I couldn't imagine what evidence they might have on me, since I had worn gloves, and I had been careful to leave the scene with the murder weapon, and how I'd left my phone at home so they couldn't use that triangulation stuff that I'd learned about during the trial. I had also intentionally picked a dark and rainy night to confront him, which would obscure any witnesses, and I had even parked some distance away, and had left my lights off as long as I could.

In fact, I believe they never would have suspected me at all, had they not somehow discovered that I'd adopted the dead man's dog, and while this did rather complicate things for the interrogation, I still felt that it was a slim piece of evidence and not much to be fussed about.

"My friend Gordon, his wife works at a shelter. She had heard that Herbert had been put up for adoption, and I thought it would be good to bring him into a good home, given all that he'd been through."

"Just doing your civic duty, right?"

It was the young officer speaking now.

"No," I said, "I have already done that."

He looked at me funny after I said it.

"So I want to get this straight," said the older mustached officer. "Man found dead in an alley six years ago, you have his dog. Man found dead at home, you have his dog. Am I clear about that?"

I could tell that they were trying to trap me with my answers, and while I wanted to say something helpful, I didn't want to be overly helpful, and was very careful not to say something that might incriminate myself. That was when I thought about The Imaginary Close.

"Imagine if you are a dog just dropped off at the shelter, and you are scared and lonely?"

Neither man responded to that, so I thought I might have done a good job of at least giving them something else to think about. Then I thought that I might also be able to incorporate The Benjamin Franklin Close.

"Perhaps we could make a list of the pros and cons to adopt a shelter dog?"

They were seemingly not inclined to do this. Not only because neither officer reached for a piece of paper, but because the younger officer slammed his palms down onto the table and yelled, "Do you think this is a fucking game?"

"No," I said.

For whatever reason, as angry as they were, I was not particularly scared in that moment. My parents had always told me that it was important to stand by your convictions, and that even if that sometimes meant that you would get in trouble, or life would be hard, that it was worth it to stay true to yourself, even if that brought about consequences. Of course, I couldn't imagine that they meant any of this to condone murder, or some of the other things that I had done in life, but I still felt it was a good lesson, all things considered.

"Fuck this guy."

That was again the young officer with the suspenders. He had just stepped away from the table as the mustached officer took his place. This time he was holding an envelope in his hand. He removed some photographs from the envelope and placed them down on the table.

"One of the neighbors had a video camera. We have you on video, walking up to his house."

It wasn't much of a surveillance image. The picture was dark and grainy, and you could tell it was raining because of how blurry it looked, and that it was taken from some distance, but at least they had used a high quality photo stock paper, so at least that much was good.

"That's you there, isn't it?" said the older officer.

I knew it was me, of course, but I equally knew that they couldn't be sure of it, because of the distance and the poor picture quality, which was clearly why they were trying to trick me into admitting that it was me. It was all very clever, and good police work.

"Who is to say who that might be?"

"So you're not denying it?" he said.

He was trying to trap me with my answers.

"It is impossible to recognize this person from this photograph," is all I said in reply.

"You think if we get a warrant, we'll find these beige pants in your house?"

"I believe that you might find several pairs of such pants," I said, "in every house in town."

It was true that it appeared the man in the photograph appeared to be wearing beige colored pants, but it was also true that it was such a common article of clothing, and clearly they knew it too, because they hadn't actually obtained a warrant to search my house, and probably didn't even have grounds to do so. What I also realized is that they were just hoping I would crack under the pressure of the questions and suddenly blurt out something incriminating, or perhaps even an outright confession. Only I wasn't like most people, because I usually liked to talk as little as possible, especially with people that I didn't much know or care about, which was the vast number of people I met in life, including these two.

"Can you account for your actions that night?"

"Which night?" I said, because I recognized they hadn't actually said the date. This was a police tactic that was sometimes used in order to trick a suspect into incriminating themselves.

I saw the mustached officer smile when I said it, and then he said, "Didn't we say what night?" and I quickly responded that he hadn't.

After another ten minutes of this, there came a knock on the door. The mustached officer answered it, and it was only a moment later that he came back in and told me I was free to go. He said it in such a polite and respectful manner, which I thought was very professional of him, given that he suspected me of being involved with Mr. Baker's death.

I rose to my feet and said, "Thank you for your service," and while the mustached officer managed a polite nod in response, the young officer said, "Get the fuck out of my face," so that is what I decided to do.

Chapter 17

I had only just stepped outside when I heard my name called aloud. That's when I saw the English detective, who was leaning against the police station.

"Well now, what say you Sonny Jim?"

"You did this?" I said as he came forward, stopping just a few feet away from me. He got a puzzled look in his face after I asked it, but it didn't seem all the way puzzled.

"And just what exactly is it that you think I've done, mate?"

"You told these police officers to question me, about Mr. Baker."

"Reckon I'm behind the chinwag, eh? Well now, what would make you suggest such a thing, Sonny Jim? You surely are a suspicious mate, aren't you? That's what I thought when I first met you, that there's a good suspicious mate if I ever saw one."

"I do not believe that it is a coincidence that you are standing out here, just as my interrogation is concluded," I said.

"Interrogation, you say? Surely it was nothing all that serious?"

"I believe that you know what just took place, and may have even helped to arrange it."

While at first it seemed like he might deny it, a smile soon curled up on his lips, then he touched his nose with his forefinger before pointing it in my direction.

"Right on the mark again, Sonny Jim. Quick as an arrow this one!"

"I wish that you would leave me alone," I said.

"Reckon you would mate, I reckon that you'd be right chuffed about it, if I left you alone. Chuffed to bits, even. Only might not be too good for the population though, you being set free that way, after pulling a good blinder on me mates here. There's a good Sonny Jim, pulling a good blinder on me mates. Bet it was a real codswallop."

I didn't understand half of what he'd just said.

"Bet you played the bog-standard," he continued, "only thing is, seems people fall off the planet that get too close to you. Maybe just an unhappy coincidence, eh mate? There's a good mate, with an unhappy coincidence."

I wasn't sure if it was a question, but even if it was, I felt that I shouldn't answer, not only because I didn't have a good one, but because I knew that they were not coincidences at all. That was when his tone suddenly sifted into something more sinister, and even if it wasn't all the way sinister, I felt there was still enough sinister in it to call it that.

"You reckon you can outlast me, mate?"

I asked him what he meant by it.

"Oh, I think you can put your finger on it, if you try. There's a good mate, putting his finger on it, if he tries to."

"I believe that you are harassing me," I said, and I believed it to be true, only I couldn't say it with too much umbrage, because I recognized that he was merely doing his job, and that he was right to be suspicious of my involvement in the deaths of these people, since it wasn't so much suspicion as actual fact that I had murdered them. Of course, he couldn't be sure of it or I'd have already been arrested, so I felt it was rather presumptuous of him to be casting about these aspersions.

"Harassment? Oh my, I hadn't thought of it that way. Your cohort, at the gala, he suggested the same thing a while back. Mortified to think of it that way, mate. Just mortified."

He did not seem mortified by it. Not then, and not now. Then I said it.

"Well mate, ruins me to hear it. Just ruins me. Of course, I'm just an honest bobbie trying to do my job. Don't want my hand to shake when I reach for my pay. That's what my father used to say, 'don't let your hand shake when you reach for your pay.' I'm sure you understand, eh mate? There's a good understanding mate."

He was being friendly again, but I felt it wasn't a sincere friendly. I also felt that no good could come of this continued conversation, and if I felt that way about most people in my day to day societal interactions, I felt it was particularly true when applied to a police detective investigating me for cold blooded murder.

I turned away from him and started walking down the steps of the police station toward my car. That was when his mood again changed away from friendly.

"You best bet we'll be watching you, Sonny Jim."

Still I didn't respond. I just walked briskly to my car. And even though I didn't turn around, and didn't have any heightened senses like Gordon did, I knew he was still there, staring at me as I went.

I could almost feel it.

Chapter 18

Up to this point in my life, I had generally been able to navigate my way through various encounters with the police, only now, having committed four murders in the last six years, I felt as if my luck was bound to run out.

I'd thought I might have been past it all, the murdering, that is. Only now that I'd killed two people in recent months, one in mostly self-defense and another that was fairly pre-meditated, I felt that it was an issue that I should probably address.

The fact was that if the neighbors surveillance cameras had been just a little closer and clearer, I might well have already been charged with Mr. Baker's murder, with the prosecutor asking the witnesses, "What happened next?" over and over and over until my own verdict came in, and how no combination of closing strategies would possibly talk the jury out of it. And though I knew it was important that I stay true to my convictions, I recognized equally that those same convictions sometimes brought about terrible consequences, and how any moment I might overlook a piece of evidence or some other fact that would link me to my crimes.

That's when I thought about Donna and Toby and Molly and Herbert, and to a lesser extent the cat, and how by living by my principles and convictions I stood a real risk of being incarcerated for life, or perhaps even made red and open if they brought back capital punishment, and how then Donna would have to fend for herself to pay all the bills, and how the family would likely struggle, how she'd likely never get her viola fixed again for as long as she lived.

But most of all I thought about how Toby would grow up without a father, and it made me think of my own father, and how much he shaped me into the person I had become, and how even if some people might think that he didn't do such a good job given some of the things that I'd done, how I knew that things would have been so much worse without him. And in that moment, driving back from the police station, I vowed to do something about it.

I arrived home well before Donna and Toby, so I took Molly and Herbert for a walk, stopping on occasion to bend down and nuzzle their chins. I could still see the scar on Herbert, where his tooth had been knocked out, only he didn't seem to mind, especially as I massaged his chin and told him he was a good boy, which of course he certainly was.

I was quite tired by the time I got back inside, so I decided to adjourn upstairs for some rest before Donna and Toby got home, only while my body was willing to adjourn, my mind was still obsessing about all the things that had happened, and all of the things that I had done. And I had only just started thinking about what I was going to do about it when I thought back to my childhood, and how whenever I acted out in a bizarre or violent fashion, that my teachers or principals or parents would have me speak with a counselor, and how my counselors had taught me various tricks and strategies to control my violent, scary thoughts. And I figured how their lessons might finally be wearing off since it had been so long—and at least four murders—since I had seen one.

That's when I thought about The Now Or Never Close, which was my brain creating a sense of urgency to act now or suffer the consequences, so I decided then and there that my best chance to remain a free man was to sit down with my own psychiatrist, psychologist, or otherwise educated person, and to see if they could help me to find a more lawful, pro-social way to deal with my urges—because I knew I could be a better person—so that is what I decided to do.

And something about this decision must have appeased my brain, because after I'd resolved to be a better person, the obsessing went away. And then finally, just as I drifted off to sleep, I realized that it had adjourned, too.

The End

Next Release

THE INTROVERT FINDS HIS FREUD

With police investigations swirling around him, the introvert decides to consult a psychiatrist, psychologist, or otherwise educated person, unearthing disturbing memories of his youth long repressed…

About the Author

Michael Paul Michaud is an author and lawyer in the Greater Toronto Area. An American-Canadian citizen, he holds a B.A. in English, Honors B.A. in Political Science (summa cum laude), and a J.D. in Law. He also makes regular appearances on SiriusXM Radio's "Canada Talks."

The Introvert Bears Filthy Witness is Michael's fourth release. His debut novel—Billy Tabbs (& The Glorious Darrow) was published in November 2014 by Bitingduck Press.

His other novels in this series include The Introvert and the Introvert Confounds Innocence.

An unabashed zealot of Animal Farm, Michaud's chief literary influence is the legendary George Orwell.

www.ingramcontent.com/pod-product-compliance
Lightning Source LLC
Chambersburg PA
CBHW070948190726
48292CB00004B/1374